WORK AND PLAY

JULIA JARRETT

CONTENTS

Chapter One

Finn

Walking through the field of young vines, my feet crunching on the frosty ground, I feel my soul travel thousands of kilometers away, to a vineyard in the hills of Alsace, France. It's a place that holds a lot of special memories for me, and the place where my grandfather now rests.

Almost there, Papa. I will make our wine soon.

When I reach the row of grapes that are the special varietal I transplanted from my grandfather's winery, which my uncle now runs, I stop and crouch to the ground. These shoots are tough, cold resistant, and hardy. They'll produce some stunning wines, but not for a few years. That's okay, though. There's a bounty of beautiful grapes in British Columbia, and thanks to my partner's contacts in the industry, we have access to some top-grade juice produced in one of the most successful vineyards in the Okanagan. Not to mention the orchards and berry fields located just down the road from where I stand that will allow us to create the custom fruit wines that are in such high demand.

"I thought I might find you out here." Pierre's faint accent reaches me and I stand to turn and face him. La Lune Rouge Winery is both of our dreams come true. For him as a business-man with a passion for wine, and for me as a winemaker. I spent several years in California honing my skills as a vintner and som-melier at some of the top wineries in Napa Valley. I won multi-ple awards for my employers and was creating a solid reputation. The work was good, but it wasn't what I wanted. When Pierre, a well-known, powerful investor in the British Columbia wine industry reached out, asking me to be his minority partner and master vintner in a small boutique winery on Vancouver Island, I knew I couldn't turn him down. Winemaking is in my blood, and with him running the business side of things, we can't lose. The wine industry here is growing leaps and bounds each day, and our goal of combining old-world French traditions with a modern, West Coast flair is going to make us stand out.

"You know you can always find me with the grapes."

His deep chuckle is filled with understanding. You don't go into the winemaking business without being more than a little obsessed with grapes.

"We have our meeting with the designer tomorrow. She'll turn that tasting room into something magnifique." Pierre kiss-es his fingertips, a nod to his French background. I have to work to hide my grimace. Even with Pierre contributing the majority of the financial investment, I'm very conscious of our budget.

After all, being a sommelier and vintner in California wasn't a huge money maker for me. The cost of living was so high my savings are not where I would like them to be. We wouldn't be spending money on an interior designer from the mainland if it was up to me. We can figure it out ourselves, or I'm sure my friends would help. But Pierre insists we meet this woman and see what she has to say. Still, I can't help but try once more to get him to see it my way.

"If we saved the money we would be spending on your designer, we could get another labeler or bottling machine instead."

"I know, I know. But we need to do this. Her father is an old friend and has asked us to give her a chance. Besides, you have all the machines you could want."

There are moments, few thankfully, that Pierre and I disagree. This is one of them.

"Pierre, seriously, we don't need her. The tasting room just has to be simple and classy. It doesn't take a high-priced designer to do that."

"It does if you want it done right." Pierre waves his hand at me, and I know the conversation is over. The fact is, he's majority owner of La Lune Rouge, so I can't force the issue. "We'll meet when she is in town tomorrow, and discuss the details. Now, come. I want to show you the blending room."

That perks my mood up. That's where I'll be spending most of my time, blending and balancing flavour notes into the perfect wine.

We walk the short distance to the renovated barn that now houses our blending room in a companionable silence. Despite our age difference, we've gotten along well so far; in many ways he reminds me of my Papa. Spending summers in France was what I was used to, and it wasn't until I became an adult that I realized what a luxury that was. Having been born to a Scottish father and a French mother, trips to Europe were the norm, but I treasured the weeks that I would spend with my grandfather. He instilled the passion and dedication to winemaking that I still hold all these years later.

When we reach the large building that houses the inner workings of what will soon be La Lune Rouge Winery, I pause for a minute and look up at the deep red barn. Amazing what two months of work from contractors can do. What was once a dilapidated barn now shines as a focal point for our future. I can already envision tours and tastings. Who knows, maybe someday we'll host events here.

"It will be full of the sounds of fermenting grapes soon, non?" Pierre says with a smirk.

"Grapes don't make sounds, old man."

"Not old yet."

I chuckle. For all that we tease, he's right. Pierre is in his prime out here, just as I am. The years that separate us don't matter when it comes to our passion, winemaking.

The interior of the barn takes my breath away, cheesy as that may sound. Great big steel tanks gleam in the dim light, waiting to be filled with juice.

"They finished the installation." The statement comes out with a boyish wonder that around anyone else, I would be embarrassed. But not here, not now.

"They did. To your exact specifications, might I add." Pierre claps me on the shoulder, then walks forward, deeper into the cavernous space. "Six fermenting tanks and a lab ready for all of your blending fantasies. Just as you envisioned." He widens his arms and turns back to me with a smile. "And the cellar out back will hold all the barrels and bottles you can possibly dream of."

"It's going to be amazing."

"Yes. Now I must go. There is a woman waiting for me at home, and I promised a bottle of Bordeaux to go with dinner."

That makes me smile. Pierre and his wife Renée are amazing together. True love that has lasted through the years. We've spent many evenings over the last few months sharing a meal and a bottle of wine, and I consider them like family. A good thing, considering how closely our futures are interwoven now that Pierre and I are partners.

"What is she cooking?" I ask as we zip up our jackets.

"I believe she's experimented with a new recipe. Some type of meat pie. Would you like to join us?"

I shake my head. "No, thank you. I need to head into town, I'm meeting the guys for a beer."

Pierre's lip curls in distaste, making me chuckle.

"I still do not understand how you can drink that terrible stuff."

"And I don't understand when you're going to stop being a snob and try some of the good beers I've sampled. We live in Canada, you know, incredible craft beer is everywhere."

"And you call yourself a sommelier."

We both laugh at that. Pierre has teased me about my enjoyment of a good beer ever since we first met and I ordered a local lager instead of wine. He couldn't understand how a professional sommelier and vintner could choose a drink other than wine, and thus began our ongoing debate.

When we go back outside, a freezing rain has started to fall. Winter over here isn't the snow-filled wonderland people expect from Canada. No, the West Coast gets slush, rain, the occasional snow fall that cripples entire cities, and more rain. I glance up at the covered walkway I insisted on installing that connects the tasting room and storefront to the barn that houses the workhorses of the operation.

"Now do you see why this makes sense?" I ask, gesturing up. Having recently moved from the interior of the province, where the climate is far harsher with hotter summers and colder winters, Pierre just grunts. He doesn't hide his distaste for the wetter weather.

We reach the tasting room, which is really only a shell of a building at present, nothing more than four walls and a roof. For now, we're using it as a pseudo-office space, with a table and four chairs being the only furniture inside. At one time, it may have been a house, but it has clearly been renovated before, as it's now a wide open space with surprisingly tall ceilings and plenty of windows. We lucked out that it didn't need any major structural work, but outfitting it with shelving, lighting, seating, décor — all the trappings that make a tasting room appealing to visitors — that will take money and time. Two things we are short on. Pierre might have deep pockets, but there are better things to spend money on than extravagant designs.

For now, we're producing just a few varietals that I've been able to create using equipment at another small, local winery. Now that our equipment is here, I can start to shift production on-site. But we'll still be doing a gradual opening and release, and it won't be until next year, or even the year after that until we'll have a full complement of wines out and can even consider being profitable. In my opinion, that's when we can spend the money fancying up the tasting room. For the time being, we just need to be able to open the doors, which means clean, simple, and tasteful should be the focus.

"I'll see you here tomorrow at ten to meet with Ashley. And Finn, try to stay open-minded." Pierre arches one eyebrow at me. He knows me well.

"I will, as long as it's what is best for the winery."

Picking up a folder from the table, Pierre walks over to me and claps his hand down on my shoulder. "That's all I ask."

Half an hour later, I push open the door to Hastings, the local bar, and let the warmth from inside hit me. It might be a Tuesday, but this place is busy like always. Dean Hastings, the owner, is a great guy, and he and his wife Riley just found out they're pregnant. It's high-risk because of her spinal cord injury, so I'm surprised to see him in here.

"Hey man, how's Riley?" I ask as I take a seat at the bar. He slides over a bottle of my favourite craft beer.

"She's doing good, thanks. We have a visit with the ob-gyn specialist next week which should include our first scan, and we're both really excited about it. You meeting the guys here tonight?"

I nod and swallow my first sip of cool, crisp lager. "Yeah. I guess I'm the first one, as usual."

Dean chuckles, then nods his head toward the door. "You didn't beat them by long."

I spin around and lift my beer in welcome to my friends. Ethan and I have known each other since university; I briefly dated his sister Mila. He's the mayor in town, and she runs a bakery and café that serves the best damn food I've ever tasted, and given that I spent my summers in Europe, that's saying something. With Ethan is Reid Corser, his friend from childhood and the elementary school principal. After Ethan settled down with Summer, who happens to be Mila's best friend, Reid became my partner in hitting the bars in Victoria for some fun, but lately something's changed, and he isn't as eager to go out as he used to be. I'm hoping that once the school shuts down for Christmas vacation in a week or so, he'll be less stressed. Then again, I'm not in my twenties anymore, and hitting the bars doesn't hold the same appeal for me, either. I'll never admit it, but part of me wants what Ethan has. Just not right now. For the time being, the winery is my girlfriend and gets all of my time and loving attention.

"Hey guys, is Jackson coming tonight?" I ask, standing and walking over to a table that can seat us all.

"Nah, he and Mila have something planned." Ethan drapes his jacket over a chair and settles in.

"Right. It has nothing to do with the glare you gave him when he and Mila announced they were moving in together." Reid drops down into the other chair and places two more beers on the table that he must have grabbed from Dean.

"I'm perfectly fine with their relationship and they both know it."

A bark of laughter escapes me. "Yeah, okay, dude. So you didn't punch him when he accused Mila of lying to him?"

"He fucking earned that," Ethan growls in response, tossing a glare my way. "Enough talk of my sister. Please. Can we just drink beer and talk about sports or something?"

I toss a pretzel at him from the bowl Dean gave us. The fucker catches it in his hand and pops it in his mouth.

"Show off," I tease good-naturedly.

Ethan shrugs. "You're just jealous."

Sad, but true. In more ways than one.

Chapter Two

Ashley

"I know, Dad, yes. Yes, I'll tell him you said hi. Okay. Thank you. Love you, too."

I hang up the phone and brush away an errant tear rolling down my cheek. It's dark and cold out here on the deck of the early morning ferry carrying me over to Vancouver Island, but I needed to get out of the noisy chaos of the full passenger lounge. And my father always knows what to say to help me center myself. After all, it's been just the two of us for the last thirty years. He was there through my hormonal teenage years, the angst of first love and first heartbreak, the challenge of choosing which university to attend, and the ups and downs of starting my own business as an interior designer.

And Lord knows I've needed him even more lately, embarrassing as it is to admit. It's been a spectacularly crappy two months, starting with my best friend Sarah moving to Toronto for her dream job, then a week later, I had the privilege of walking in on my boyfriend of almost two years fucking another woman in our bed. I probably should have suspected something when he wanted to move in together, but also asked for one night a week of 'alone time.' At the time it seemed like a great idea. A perfect opportunity for me to have some time with my dad, and for him to catch up with the boys. Little did I know that while Dad and I were having dinner or playing chess, Tyson was busy banging his way through the city of Vancouver. Granted, that relationship wasn't exactly amazing...the sex was mediocre at best, and Tyson never did accept the fact that I'm not an openly affectionate person. I don't run around hugging everyone immediately. He always accused me of being rude when his friends' girlfriends would try to hug me, but for crying out loud, I didn't even know them.

Anyway, finding him in our bed with another woman was almost a relief. It was the ending to something that I should have walked away from a lot sooner. Kicking him out was cathartic in a way. But one thing became abundantly clear, I had to move. No way could I stay in that apartment a moment longer, knowing he had done who-knows-what with who-knows-who there.

Dad was happy to have me move in with him, and I had hoped it would be a short-term solution while I looked for another apartment not tainted by Tyson's activities. However, my search has lasted a lot longer than I wanted, thanks to the viciously expensive and competitive rental market in Vancouver.

To add insult to injury, business has been slow going on half a year now. It doesn't matter that I have multiple awards behind me and several successful businesses willing to recommend me. The need for interior designers of my style is low right now. The casual, yet luxurious, boho-chic vibe that I am known for isn't what the downtown clients want anymore. Which means my options are to either completely change my design style or look for work elsewhere.

Which brings me here. On a boat, headed to a winery that an old friend of my dad owns. I've spent my entire career doing everything I can to *not* accept help from my father. It's not that he isn't willing; quite the opposite. Dad has always tried to help, offering to refer me to some of the investment clients he works for. But the trust fund he insisted on setting up for me felt like enough of a handout. Having him send work my way just didn't sit right. I needed to make my own way, not live up to the trust fund princess nickname the awful girls at my private school gave me. Still, after two months with no hints of work on the horizon, I was starting to panic. So this time, after saying *no* so many other times, when Dad offered to give my name to his friend Pierre, I had to say yes.

"You need a break, sweet pea. Some time away from this damn city and all the chaos. I see what the last few months have done to my beautiful daughter and I want to weep. Where is the gentle, fun loving, trusting soul you used to be?"

Dad's words might have stung a little, but they weren't wrong. The weight of the last few months was starting to drag me down, and I could hear a cynical, bitchy voice getting louder and louder, telling me I would never be successful, would never find real love, would never find a life that truly fit.

So I jumped on the opportunity to get away from it all. If the pitch goes well today, I could be moving to the island temporarily while I oversee the work being done. I've never pictured myself enjoying small-town life, heck, I grew up eating sushi and going to the Vancouver Symphony Orchestra with my dad. But maybe a slower pace will be good for a change.

I'm also ashamed to admit, I thought this would be an easy job for some easy money. Until, that is, I started doing my market research on tasting rooms. Because what I saw didn't exactly inspire me. It seemed every other winery either embodied the old-world, heavy wood, traditional vibe, or a very upscale, trendy, minimalist feel. I can design just about anything, but those two aesthetics are not my preferred choice. Still, experience has shown me I need to give the client what they need, which isn't always what I want. This is why my proposed design includes clean lines and a much simpler elegance than what I would prefer. It was painstaking to do, because every fiber of my design soul wanted to do something different.

I've also got a second design, not as well thought out, but far more in keeping with my typical style. The winery is called La Lune Rouge, and as soon as I heard that I was filled with ideas on how to bring that vision to life. The fact that this version will likely never see the light of day shouldn't bother me; after all, at this point, a job is a job.

I let out one more deep huff of air then slide my phone back into the pocket of my winter coat. I need coffee and something sugary to get me through the rest of this day. When I head inside, I make my way to the line up for the café on board the ferry. Once I've got my coffee in hand, I eye the prepackaged pastries. Nothing seems very appetizing, but I guess I don't have much choice.

"Don't bother with those. Depending on where you're headed, I can point you in the direction of the best muffins you've ever had."

I turn to see a beautiful blonde woman standing behind me. Her long hair is twisted into a bun on the top of her head, and she's got an air of elegance, despite her warm smile.

"I gotta admit, these look pretty gross."

She nods sympathetically. "One of my best friends has a bakery. If you're headed up island, swing into Dogwood Cove and look for The Nutty Muffin. Tell whoever's working that Serena sent you, and they'll get you one of the apple nut muffins Mila saves in the back for her friends. They're to die for, I promise."

"Good to know, thanks." I put the muffin down and move to fill up my travel mug with coffee.

"So, what brings you to the island?"

Startled, I look up again, and the blonde — Serena, I guess — is still smiling at me as she fills her mug with an herbal tea.

"Oh, umm, a possible job."

"Cool. I hope you get it, the island is an amazing place. I've lived in Dogwood Cove for the last ten years and I can't imagine being anywhere else. Anyway, I better find somewhere to sit down, I've got dance videos to critique." She rolls her eyes and walks over to the cash register with a backwards wave. "Don't forget, visit The Nutty Muffin and tell them I sent you!"

"I will," I call out as she leaves the cafeteria area. I'm not going to lie, I'm not used to strangers being that friendly. It definitely isn't like that in the city. Vancouver might be known as a friendly place, but downtown where I live and where most of my work is, it's a fast-paced hub of business. Not many people take the time to just chat with strangers like Serena just did. And ever since Sarah moved away, the city has felt even more lonely.

Once I've paid for my coffee, I make my way to a window seat, and for the next half hour, I manage to zone out, scrolling through my phone. I have a small obsession with profession-al athletes, and let me tell you, the Instagram feeds for the Nashville Fury football team and the Atlanta Rising soccer team are highly enjoyable. Whoever is running those social media accounts deserves a raise. Then again, maybe taking pictures and videos of sweaty, half naked athletes is bonus enough.

When the announcement comes for passengers to return to their cars, I reluctantly shut off my phone and gather my things. It's a short drive to Dogwood Cove, and I factor in a few extra minutes to swing by the bakery that Serena, I think she said her name was, recommended. I could use a muffin. Or two.

As I drive off the boat and follow the long line of cars headed to the highway, I mentally go over my pitch for the winery. Even though dear old Dad organized this opportunity, I don't consider it a done deal. I've still got to win over the winery owner and get him to approve the design.

It doesn't take me long to reach the turnoff for Dogwood Cove, and even less time to find the bakery Serena mentioned. I'm charmed by the adorable small-town vibe the main street has with its well-kept store fronts, town square, with a freaking gazebo right in the middle. Seriously, it's like Stars Hollow leapt off the small screen and into real life.

The door lets out a charming sound when I push it open, and the young guy behind the counter smiles in welcome.

"Welcome to The Nutty Muffin. What can I get you?"

I peruse the contents of the gleaming glass case that is filled with so many delicious-looking things my mouth is instantly watering. "I was told the apple nut muffins were the thing to ask for."

His face falls into an apologetic frown. "I'm sorry, we're sold out for today. If you come back early tomorrow we'll have another batch."

"Oh, nuts." I fidget with my hands before remembering what Serena said. "I ran into a woman named Serena on the ferry over here. She's the one who told me about them, but I won't be here tomorrow. Next time, I guess."

He winks. "Well, if Serena sent you, that's different. Hang on, honey."

*I can't believe that worked...*I guess small towns really are different.

He comes bustling back out with a small paper bag that he hands over to me with a smile. "Here you go. One secret stash apple nut muffin for Serena's new friend."

I take the bag and reach for my wallet. "Wow, thank you. What do I owe you?"

"Now take a bite and tell me it's the best muffin you've ever eaten and consider that payment. And when you come back for more, which you will, trust me, just ask for Sebastian. That's me, and I'll make sure you're hooked up."

My jaw drops. "What? No. I can't take it for free, I barely know Serena, she just spoke to me on the ferry and recommended this place and —"

"Serena is one of my best friends. If she told you to mention her name in exchange for a muffin, it's because she liked you." A beautiful, dark-haired woman comes out of the kitchen, dusting her hands off on an apron. "I'm Mila, this is my bakery. Welcome to Dogwood Cove." Her greeting is warm and inviting, and automatically brings an answering smile to my face.

"Hi, and thank you. Your café is amazing. But really, I don't mind paying for the muffin."

Mila waves her hand at me, then hands over the coffee Sebastian passes to her. "Nope, not happening. Serena is a good judge of character, and a die-hard fan of my muffins. She wanted you to have it, so please take it."

I finally give in to what feels like a losing battle over a muffin and take a bite. "Ohmgd." The mumbled words come out before I can even think about how rude it is to speak with food in my mouth. Once I've swallowed down the bite of the most delicious thing I've ever eaten, I look back up at Mila who's standing there with a smug smirk.

"This is incredible."

"Yep. I'm famous for them. So. What's your name, what brings you to Dogwood Cove, where are you from, where are you staying?"

"Uh-umm," I stammer out. I'm not used to this level of aggressively friendly interaction with strangers, but Mila is just looking at me expectantly. "Ashley, I'm here to consult on a design project, I'm from Vancouver, and I'm not staying. Just here for the day."

Mila drops her elbows down to the counter and props her head in her hands. "Ooh. Tell me more, Ashley from Vancouver. What's the project? No wait. Let me guess. Is it a new B&B? No, I would've heard of that. Umm...hmm. Is it for a store?"

"It's for a winery? La Lune Rouge. My, ah, my dad knows the guy who's opening it, so..." my voice trails off lamely as I realize how immature and unprofessional it sounds to admit that I only have this opportunity thanks to my father.

"Oh my God, I know Finn, one of the owners! That's incredible. The wine is so damn good. What are you designing?"

Mila is happy and friendly, and it almost makes me feel like she doesn't care how I got the job. She is simply genuinely interested in me. It's weird, unsettling almost, to be the focus of that attention. Definitely not what I'm used to.

"The tasting room and wine shop."

"Oh you're an interior designer? That is so cool! Hey, what do you think of this place? I admit, I did it myself to save money, but I like it."

"You did it all yourself? Wow, you've got great taste." I take another look around, absorbing the way the warm colour palette blends together without being boring, the comfortable furniture, and strategic lighting that highlights what appears to be local artwork for sale on the walls. "I mean it, Mila. This place is beautiful. It's exactly my style. Casual, but cozy and well pulled together. It's inviting and interesting. I'm impressed." When I turn back to her with a smile, she looks inordinately pleased.

"That is so nice of you to say. Wow. A real designer likes my style. Wait 'til I tell my older brother. He's always trying to get me to fancy the place up, but I keep telling him — people like comfort with their coffee."

I giggle. "Exactly. If I wanted boring, I would go to Tim Hortons."

Mila delicately shudders. "Boring and gross. Their donuts don't hold a candle to my homemade fritters. Next time you're in town I'll whip up a batch. I'm guessing you'll be here again if you're working on the winery?"

"I guess, but I don't have the job yet. Just an interview, sort of." I glance at my phone to check the time. "Shoot, I've got to go. Thank you again for breakfast." I give Mila a grateful smile, and on my way out, I tuck a twenty dollar bill into the jar on the counter that has a sign attached, indicating tips will go toward donations for the food bank.

"See you next time, Ashley!" Mila calls out to me and I turn to give her a wave, only to bump into someone on my way out the door.

"Oh my God, I'm so sorry!" I cry out as strong hands grip my waist, steadying me. I'm so busy checking my blouse for coffee that I don't look up until the smooth but playful voice hits me.

"It's all good, no coffee was sacrificed. And I should have been watching where I was going."

My eyes dart up and meet the most vibrant green eyes I've ever seen on a man. The scruff he's sporting doesn't hide the strong jawline, or the dimple I see peeking through. A backwards ball cap completes the trifecta of sexiness. As my gaze travels unabashedly over his face, I realize I'm still standing in the doorway, and I need to find my way to the winery for my meeting.

"Shit. Sorry. No. I mean, yes. I mean, I have to go."

I push past the most handsome man I've ever seen, inwardly cursing my apparent lack of social skills. Of course I meet mister tall, dark, and scruffy — basically my kryptonite of a man — on the day I have no time, too much stress, and not enough caffeine to function.

Once I'm back at my car, I allow myself to take a long sip of coffee. The liquid is hot, but not too hot, and I can feel the warmth filling me against the chill outside.

Okay. Must stop thinking about hot men and start thinking about presenting to old men.

I can do this. I can impress the crap out of these winery owners. Even if it does mean spending more time over here, instead of hustling for clients in the city.

Who knows? Maybe I'll even see mister tall, dark, and scruffy again.

And maybe next time I'll manage to *not* make a total fool out of myself.

CHAPTER THREE

Finn

Not gonna lie, that was a nice surprise. I casually turn and watch the woman who bumped into me walk away. I never thought pencil skirts were my thing, but turns out when they're paired with tall boots and curves for days, I can appreciate them. And I wouldn't normally notice a woman's hair, but when it cascades halfway down her back in gorgeous golden waves, well, all I can picture is running my hands through it, gripping it tightly and...

"Finn McNeil, stop drooling and get in here. You're letting the heat out."

I turn toward Mila's voice with a wolfish grin. "Who, me? Drool? Never."

She rolls her eyes and hands over a cup of coffee. The perk of being good friends with a café owner? She knows my order and has it ready each morning. "Thanks, gorgeous. What'll it take for you to tell me who the beautiful coffee girl is that I happened to bump into?"

Mila brings her hands to her hips, and an enigmatic smile lighting up her face. "I'm not going to tell you."

"What? Why not?"

"Because. It'll do you some good to not have *everything* you want just handed to you on a silver platter."

"That doesn't happen," I scoff, and Mila arches an eyebrow at me. "Okay, fine. Don't tell me. I'll figure it out myself."

"Yes, I think you will," comes her cryptic reply.

I slip some money into the jar Mila uses to collect tips, except, instead of sharing them amongst staff, they donate the money to local charities.

"See ya, Mills." My parting shot includes the nickname Ethan gave to his sister, which she happens to hate, making it the perfect retaliation for right now.

"Don't you start, or you'll lose coffee privileges."

I raise my hand in surrender as I back up to the door. I'm not messing with my coffee. Without it I won't make it through a day. Mila's coffee is the best and she knows it, which makes it a highly effective blackmail tactic. "Okay, okay, sorry. Have a good day, Mila."

Outside on the sidewalk, I take a sip of coffee and then a bite of the cinnamon scone I chose to go with it. Both are amazing. Mila and I tried dating for a while when we were younger, but it was quickly apparent we made better friends. And thank fuck for that because it's bad enough having this easy access to her baking. If we were together, I would have to dramatically increase my fitness program to keep up. And going for a run with the guys or hitting the gym a few times a week is all I really care to do right now.

I zip my jacket up higher against the chill in the air. It's cold today, but the skies are clear, thankfully. That means tonight will be even colder for the Christmas tree lighting. When Ethan first told me this was a thing, I laughed at him. I couldn't believe any town would be so cliché. But he insisted it was a thing, then went on to tell me that this year there would be real fucking animals in some sort of live nativity scene. The whole idea seems ridiculous to me — small-town charm? More like small-town cheese. But I have to admit, Dogwood Cove has this way of sucking you in and making you never want to leave. It's not just that we're in what has to be one of the most beautiful places on earth, with oceans, mountains, lakes, and rivers — everything nature has to offer at our doorstep. It's also the people. Everyone is so damn friendly and welcoming. Turner, at the hardware store, has been a huge help ordering in specialty parts that our contractor needed for the winery. All of the local restaurants have already agreed to start serving La Lune Rouge wines once we're up and running. And so many residents have come up to me to tell me how excited they are for the winery to open.

Honestly, it was overwhelming when I first moved here. I couldn't believe a place like this really existed outside of Hallmark movies.

My phone starts to ring, interrupting me from my rambling thoughts. When I see my mom's name on it, I smile. Yeah, I'm a total mama's boy.

"Hey Mom, how's it goin'?"

"Mon cher, how are you?" Mom's French accent settles over me. Our weekly phone calls are a constant in my life, and I wouldn't trade it for anything.

"Good, Mom. Just headed out to meet with Pierre. He's got someone coming today to discuss design ideas for the tasting room."

"Ah, that will be wonderful. You're so close to opening, no?"

"Yeah, just a few more months. But this isn't the real opening. Just a soft one. Until we start making all of our wines on the premises, I won't consider it open."

She tsks me in that way only mothers can. "Finn. You have realized your dream. Why will you not let yourself acknowledge that?"

"Because we aren't a real winery until it's *my* tanks that are filled with fermenting juice."

I know she's rolling her eyes at me, and the truth is, Pierre does the same thing. Neither one of them understand that for me, the dream is to make my own wine on my own land. Only then will I consider myself a true winery owner. I don't discount how lucky we are to be able to use our grapes and make wine using equipment at another site, but it isn't the same. It's a temporary solution and one I hope will be unnecessary very soon.

"Fine, my stubborn boy. I won't argue. You get that from your father, you know, that steel resolve." Her voice is laced with love for both me and my dad. Their marriage is one for the ages.

"Yeah, I know," I say with a smile as I unlock my truck and climb in, turning on the engine to warm up the cab. My mother's voice fills the truck when my phone switches to Bluetooth, and I put the truck in drive to start heading out to the winery.

"When do you arrive for Christmas, mon cher?"

"The twenty-third. And before you ask, no, I can't stay longer than a week."

"Fine, fine. I'll take what I can get. I had better go, your father has made omelettes for breakfast. Je t'aime mon cher."

"Love you too, Mom."

I hang up the phone and turn onto the road that leads outside of town where the winery is located. Just down the road from us is the turnoff to Oceanside Resort, which is owned by Ethan's fiancée Summer. It's a really cool place, and she's spent a lot of time and effort cleaning it up. She opened in August and has had every weekend booked steadily.

When I get to the winery, Pierre's car is already there, but I don't see another vehicle, and I realize I've got a few minutes to try and convince him to keep costs down and skip the designer. Sure, we'll meet with her, but I know how much Pierre has invested in this place and how much I have. And let's just say if I want to keep things even remotely even, we can't afford any more major costs. Correction, *I* can't afford for us to have any more major costs.

Inside the empty tasting room, Pierre is seated at the table with what I know is an almond milk latte in front of him.

"Morning," I say as I hang up my coat.

"I was worried you would not make it in time; Ashley took a wrong turn and is running late. Which I suppose is a good thing, since now we have a few moments before she arrives." Pierre takes off his glasses and looks at me studiously. "I know you're worried about things."

I sit down slowly, uncertain where he's going with this.

"When I asked you to be my partner, I knew that I was asking you to take on more of the work that will happen once we are open and running. I also knew that I would be taking on more of the financial burden leading up to that point. My beautiful wife pointed out to me last night that perhaps you needed a small reminder of that. And perhaps you need to hear me say I still consider you my partner, even if I am writing the cheques."

A heavy silence hangs between us. He's right, or I should say, Renée is right. Even though the rational part of me can recognize that our original agreement entailed him fronting most of the money, and me handling most of the hands-on work. This will allow him to step back as a silent investor once we're up and running. It's hard for me to remember that I'm still considered his partner.

"I suppose it is hard to remember that sometimes," I reply slowly. "It's not that I don't appreciate our agreement; you've given me an opportunity I would have never realized on my own. But it's important to me to feel that I'm pulling my weight, you know?"

Pierre lets out a small sound of agreement.

I straighten in my chair, leaning forward to rest my elbows on my knees. If I truly am his partner, then I need to say my piece. "Regardless of who's paying for what, or who is doing what work, the fact remains that we don't need a fancy tasting room right now. Not until we have a full compliment of wines available, not until we decide about the bistro idea, just *not now*. All we need is something clean, simple, and classy. And I still maintain that we don't need a designer for that."

Pierre leans back in his chair, nodding his head. "A valid opinion, and one I do respect. Truly. Yet simple does not stand out. Simple does not make a statement. And we want to make a statement, do we not? People will not come to see us if we do not give them a reason to. Why, when they can buy the wine in a store, would they travel to the winery, if we do not stand out as a destination? Do you not remember visiting the other wineries with me? They were simple and classy. They were boring. La Lune Rouge will not be boring."

When he finishes his speech, I know I'm fighting a losing battle. And I have to grudgingly accept he has a good point.

"No, it won't be boring," I acquiesce. "But just tell me you agree — it doesn't have to cost us a fortune to make a statement."

Pierre raises his eyebrows at me over his latte and shrugs his shoulders. "We will see what Ashley says. We need to be open-minded with her, Finn."

I open my mouth in a last-ditch effort to make my stubborn partner understand when the door opens, effectively ending our conversation.

"I'm so sorry I'm late, these roads are not well marked and I just got so turned around."

That voice makes my dick stir in my pants.

It's her. Coffee girl.

And seeing her up close again only reinforces for me how fucking beautiful she is. She's got the girl next door vibe going on, and the combination of her looks paired with that sexy skirt and blouse combo makes me sit up straighter. Her long hair isn't down anymore, now it's wrapped up in some kind of twist, and it shows off the column of her neck perfectly. I can tell the instant she recognizes me. Her eyes widen and she tugs her lower lip between her teeth. Damn.

Pierre stands up and goes to greet her with a kiss to each cheek. Huh, interesting, she doesn't like his French greeting, the discomfort at his touch is evident. "Ashley, it is so wonderful to see you again. It has been too many years. Don't worry about being late, Finn and I were just discussing a few things."

Her mouth falls open when he says my name. Well. Before I can wonder why she had that reaction, it comes to me. Mila. That woman likes to talk, and given our first run in was as Ashley was leaving the café, and *especially* given Mila's reluctance to tell me anything about her...I'm willing to bet Mila told Ashley I worked at the winery.

Maybe using a designer for the space won't be as much of an issue as I worried it would be. It might be an asshole move, but I'll use her obvious attraction to me to my advantage. Get her to go along with my idea of a simple design and a low budget.

But then she leans over to set her bag down and I'm given the slightest glimpse of the curve of her breasts, and goddamn, is that lace?

Work with her? No problem. It'll be keeping my hands off her that will be more difficult.

Chapter Four

Ashley

You have *got* to be kidding me. Mister tall, dark, and scruffy is Finn? The Finn that Mila said owns the winery? Shit, shit, shit, shit. I was expecting a couple of old men, not the hottie I made a fool of myself in front of. There goes any sense of cool, calm, and collected I thought I had harnessed.

Okay, so the other man, Pierre, who's supposedly a friend of my dad, is older. And a lot friendlier and less stuffy than I thought he would be. I could have done without his effusive greeting, but he caught me off guard before I could put out a hand to shake to ward off his embrace.

I don't do hugs. Or kisses on the cheek. It's nothing personal, I'm just not a big fan of being affectionate with random people. And yes, I know, Pierre isn't random. I've technically known him for a long time, but the last time I saw the man, I think I was a teenager.

"It's nice to see you, too, Pierre. Thank you for this opportunity." I carefully avoid Finn's penetrating gaze, but I feel it. Oh

Lordy, do I feel it. I take the folder holding my design ideas out of my bag, but of course as luck would have it, the page where I sketched out my personal thoughts and ideas comes flying out with it. My face is flaming, I'm sure, as I scramble to put things down and get it out of sight, but I'm too late.

"These colours. Ashley, this is beautiful. Is this part of your plan?" Pierre's eyes are scanning the single sheet of paper that is cringeworthy in terms of how unprofessional it is. I hurry to try and cover my tracks.

"Oh, no, no, no. That was just some silly playing around while I was on the ferry." I open the folder that holds the dad-approved design plan, the one that's soft shades of grey and minimalist décor. "This is what I designed for you."

Pierre barely glances at the actual design, or the sample materials I am in the midst of laying out. When I chance a peek at Finn, his expression is unreadable. But with those crossed arms, I can tell he is not yet on board with Pierre's level of enthusiasm.

"I think not."

My heart plummets to my feet at Pierre's words until I realize that he's finally put my sketch down and is looking at the official design. He closes the folder and turns back to me.

"That is cold, sterile. I mean no offense to your talent, Ashley, because it is clear you know what you're doing. But that is not La Lune Rouge." He holds up the sketch of the boho-chic, decadent jewel tone coloured page where I had let my creativity run free. "*This* is La Lune Rouge."

I can't deny the thrill of pride and excitement I feel that it's my personal style and taste that Pierre is drawn to. The idea of bringing my ideas to life in this space excites me more than any other project I've worked on.

"I'm honoured you like my idea, Pierre. I'm just so sorry I don't have a formal design plan drawn up using those ideas. It really was just me having fun and thinking outside the box."

"Outside the box is exactly what I, what *we,* are going for." I don't miss the pointed stare Pierre gives Finn, who has so far remained silent.

"Okay...well, I can certainly fill out the design a lot more, but it will take me some time. Overall, though, especially now seeing the space, I think we can create a really intimate, luxurious space. Something that feels decadent without being over the top." My mind's eye starts seeing the room come together. Deep colours, soft textures, rich wood finishes. I start jumping ahead to sourcing, already thinking of which stores and vendors I'll reach out to when Finn's gravelly voice pierces my musings.

"I think your original design is a better idea."

His words could be complimentary, if they were said in a different tone. But when I look at him, there's a guarded expression on his face, one that says it might not be easy to get him on board with everything. And underneath it, I could swear I detect a thread of vulnerability.

Interesting.

The fact is, whatever I'm seeing intrigues me. And that could be dangerous. I need this job to turn out the best it possibly can, even if the future of my career lies on the mainland.

"Let me come back with a complete design based on this idea, and then we can discuss it further," I offer, hoping to at least get Finn on board with that.

Pierre looks at him. "That sounds reasonable, doesn't it Finn? That way we can see both ideas in their entirety before we make any decisions."

Finn folds his arms across his chest and he leans back; a shot of lust surprises me at the sight of his muscular forearms draped over his pecs. "Yeah. And can you include some budget projections, please."

A lightbulb goes off in my head. Suddenly that vulnerability makes sense. And I fight back a grin as I straighten my spine. "Of course. You should know, sustainable practice is a tenet for my work."

His expression clouds in confusion for a moment, but it's gone before I can do more than raise my eyebrows at him. Suddenly my nerves are gone, and I've got a new ambition. Show mister tall, dark, and scruffy exactly who he's dealing with.

Pierre stands up and claps his hands. "Excellent. Ashley, let's finalize a time to meet again with the two finished plans."

I stand as well. "Actually, I can finish them today if you're available to meet tomorrow?" I quickly run through what I've got in my car to make sure I have what I need to stay overnight.

Thankfully, I was ready with a spare outfit change just in case and I always have some basic toiletries with me.

A swift nod comes from Pierre at my suggestion, but Finn remains silent. "Excellent. We shall meet here again tomorrow at ten." Pierre looks down at his phone, then back to me. "Unfortunately, I must go. Finn can help you find your way to a motel in town if you like."

"I'll be fine. Thank you, Pierre, I'll see you tomorrow." I smile at the older man and start to gather my papers, making a point not to connect my gaze with Finn.

Finn stays where he is the entire time I'm packing my bag, silently watching me until I turn to leave, desperate to get away from the tense atmosphere between us. I don't know what I've done to piss him off, but the cold shoulder is not fun.

"Have you ever been to a top-tier winery, Ashley?"

Arrogance drips from every word, light-years different from the relaxed, flirtatious man I ran into at the bakery.

"Depends on what you mean by top-tier, I suppose," is my casual response. He's trying to get a rise out of me, but I'll be damned if I'm going to give in.

"We're not going for some bohemian cat café vibe here. Our clientele will expect our space to be elegant and classy. That can't be achieved with throw pillows and sconces."

I slowly put my bag back down, silently counting to ten in my head to try and maintain my calm. Who the fuck is this guy, thinking he can tell me how to do my job? Am I telling him how to make grape juice? *No I am not.*

"Finn, you obviously don't want me here. That's fine. You're not the one who hired me, Pierre is. So get over yourself."

He cocks an eyebrow at me, and a grin stretches across his face. "Get over myself? Huh. Okay, I have to admit I haven't had anyone say that to me in a while." He pushes back his chair and stands, and I suddenly realize just how close he is. Close enough for me to get a whiff of his cologne, a decidedly masculine scent that makes me think of all the finer things in life, wrapped up in one deliciously wicked package. "Look, Ashley. It's not that I don't want you here, it's that I don't think we *need* you here. Yet, here you are. I'll *play nice* with you, as long as you remember that at the end of the day, this job might be temporary for you, but it can have permanent impacts for us. We need it done right."

Again that flash of vulnerability shows itself. And softens me against his hard edges.

"I get it, Finn. I want this to be a success. For me, and for you."

He nods. "Okay. So, tomorrow."

"Tomorrow."

As soon as I get back to the motel I'm staying in tonight, I change out of my formal clothes and into the yoga pants and tank top I had in my car, courtesy of a class I never ended up making the day before I came here. *Thank God I work for myself,* is all I can think as I survey the spread of my materials on the bed. Carrying around a selection of materials, as well as my sketchbook, laptop, and design software is part of my normal routine, which makes this last minute designing a lot easier than it could have been.

I may not have everything I would want for a full-scale design pitch, but I think I've got enough to show Pierre and Finn the two ideas, and just for Finn, I've included some rough budgets. The thought of showing him what I can do in terms of repurposed materials and thrift store finds makes me smile in anticipation. I'll hopefully be able to satisfy Pierre's design dreams along with Finn's budget worries and come out with a signed contract in the end.

The thing is, the way I do my job is very hands-on, meaning I'll need to temporarily relocate to Dogwood Cove for a couple of months. That in and of itself is not necessarily a bad thing, given my lack of a living situation back in the city. No self-respecting girl my age wants to still be living with their father. Where things get complicated is with Finn. There's no sense in denying the fact that I'm attracted to him, even if he doesn't exactly want me here. But I can't let myself get distracted by him.

Because he looks like he works hard and plays harder.

If only I were here to play, not work.

My phone interrupts my wicked thoughts of Finn with an incoming video call from Sarah. I open the app and settle back against the headboard. "Hey girly, how's T-dot?"

Sarah's curly hair is wild around her face as she smiles back at me. "Oh my God, boo. It's nuts here. The art scene is incredible."

Sarah got her dream job working at an art gallery as an acquisitions expert. She's putting her fancy arts degree to use and loving every minute of it. A pang of jealousy hits me, but disappears quickly. I'm working my dream job as well, it just isn't going quite so well at the moment.

"Tell me all about the winery. Did they love your soul sucking design?"

I roll my eyes dramatically. "Oh my God. Nope, they did not." I pause for effect, and burst out laughing when Sarah starts to curse. "Hang on, hang on. It's fine. The owner, Pierre, he saw the sketch I showed you of how I would design the space if it were mine. Remember the one full of reds and golds? He loved *that* design," I finish triumphantly.

"Yes! Naturally, your style wins the day. I am so proud of you, boo!"

My heart fills with affection and longing. "I miss you, Sarah."

"Oh man, I miss you, too. It's just not the same being out here without you."

I fall silent at that reminder. At one point we planned to move to Toronto together someday. But my dad had a health scare two years ago, and I realized I couldn't leave British Columbia. Being on the other side of the country, away from my one remaining family member was too scary.

"I know. I wish I was there," I say quietly.

"It's all good," Sarah says gamely. "You're gonna take the winery world by storm with your tasting room designs, and I'm gonna be the best art dealer Toronto has ever seen. And once a year we'll meet up in some crazy tropical destination for a girls week. Deal?"

"Deal."

When we get off the phone an hour later, I'm feeling ready to win Finn and Pierre over tomorrow. Sarah's always known how to get my head out of whatever spiral I'm in, and focus in on what's really important. Her eye for art and design helped me put the finishing touches on what I'm planning, and I go to bed knowing that whatever happens, I'm committed to making this project turn out amazing.

Chapter Five

Finn

My AirPods do a bad job of drowning out the noise of the crowded lounge on the ferry that carries me to the mainland. Traveling at Christmas is the worst, and if I hadn't sunk so much money into the winery I would have sprung for a float plane to take me home instead of this boat packed with families traveling for the holiday. At least I managed to get a window seat, and the older man beside me is quiet, content to read his paper. I'm trying to take advantage of the forced downtime by scrolling through news headlines on my phone, but no matter what I do, my fucking thoughts keep drifting back to Ashley. The initial excitement I felt over seeing her walk into the room at the winery for the first time faded quickly when it became apparent that her presence was going to cause a hit to my wallet that I really can't afford. And even the next day, when she came back with a more complete plan, lust and anxiety continued to do battle inside of me. She might be the sexiest woman I've laid eyes on in a long time, she might smell like the richest bouquet of flowers, but those sketches she showed us, and the samples she pulled up on her laptop while we chatted screamed *expensive* to me. And Pierre's excitement and enthusiasm only spurred her on. I tried to keep what he said in my mind — he's there for the bulk of the financial investment because he recognizes that the bulk of the actual work of running the winery, and making the wine of course, will fall on me. That should make me feel better about the rising costs, but it doesn't. I want to pay my way, at least as much as it takes to maintain the 60-40 split of investment, ownership, and eventual profit that Pierre and I agreed upon when we first came to our partnership. And I just can't seem to shake the sinking feeling that Ashley's decadent design is going to force my forty percent to be a hell of a lot more money than I initially intended it to be.

I pull up the document that holds the digital version of her design and open it again. It's not that I don't like her idea. I'll admit it — I do. It's beautiful, and her talent is astounding. Now seeing it in its entirety, I feel bad for my throw pillow comment the other day. She has captured the vibe of La Lune Rouge in a way even I couldn't describe. Luxurious, yet welcoming. A place that makes anyone feel spoiled, and at home, all at the same time. The rich colours she's chosen, and the textile samples she showed us, they paint a picture of a tasting room that will rise above any winery I've visited in British Columbia. It's on par with the boutique wineries in Napa that I worked at, the ones that get away with charging a fortune for tastings. But that's what scares me. I don't want to have to charge that much for people to taste my wine. I want it to be available to everyone. I want quality wine to be something all can enjoy.

She hadn't been able to give us a detailed budget projection when she first presented us with the completed plans. Which naturally heightened my discomfort. But the email from Pierre containing the budget she sent him is sitting in my inbox. I'm avoiding opening it, immature as that may seem. I don't want to spend my time with my parents agonizing over how to come up with the money needed to make her perfect vision a reality. Ignorance isn't exactly bliss, but it's better than the consuming worry I know I'll have once I prove my fears to be correct and look at the cost.

I inwardly roll my eyes at my negative perspective. This isn't me, at least it didn't used to be. Worrying more about money than about finding pleasure and happiness in everything. I'm not ashamed to admit I was sheltered, and fine — spoiled — growing up. I wanted for nothing, and as an only child my parents both doted on me. Add to that my mother's permanently upbeat attitude about life, my father's work ethic, and my grandfather's patient guidance, and I've had it good. Now that my dreams are in reach, I feel like I should be celebrating, not silently panicking.

Settling back into the cushioned seat, I close my eyes and take several deep breaths, forcing thoughts of budgets, dwindling savings, and mounting debts from my conscious mind. Unbidden, a vision of Ashley sneaks in. But without the accompanying financial dread, I see her differently. I see the sensuous curve of her hip, the luscious fall of her hair over her shoulders, and the way her plump lips taunt and tease me, begging me to kiss them. Hell, even the fire I saw in her eyes when I tried to challenge her inspiration had me ready to toss her over my shoulder like a goddamn caveman and have my way with her.

If this were any other situation, if she were anyone else in the world, I would be pursuing her. I would much rather be figuring out how to get Ashley in my bed, not fighting frustration that she could ruin me financially. But that will never happen. Not just because it's clear she's important to Pierre, but also because we'll be working together for the foreseeable future, for better or worse. I had a brief fling with one of the servers at the bistro attached to a winery I worked at one summer during university. A fling that ended in me being fired because it turned out she didn't like the fact that I wasn't interested in more than a night or two and her uncle owned the winery. I swore I'd never mix business and pleasure again. Which makes it seriously fucking frustrating that I feel like a teenager with how my libido seems to come roaring to life at just the thought of her.

Enough. It's a little ridiculous how consumed I am in equal parts with money and Ashley. It's all making me feel pathetic, and that's not an emotion I'm enjoying. I straighten up, pick up my phone again, and open the group text message between myself, Ethan, Reid, and Jackson.

FINN: Okay assholes, when I get back over there I'm instigating a monthly poker night.

JACKSON: Sounds good, man. Let's do it when the girls have their "book club"

REID: Why do you put quotes around book club…

JACKSON: Because it's definitely just a chance for them to drink lots of wine and talk about sex.

ETHAN: Dude. How many fucking times do I have to tell you not to say the word sex. I don't wanna be picturing you and my sister.

JACKSON: Right. Yeah. She's a virgin. We're totally celibate.

That makes me snort loud enough that the man next to me looks up, startled. I mouth the word sorry, and go back to the messages.

ETHAN: Fuck you.

REID: Huh. Well I'm free any night. No book club issues here.

FINN: How long are you gonna keep THAT lie going?

REID: What lie?

JACKSON: You and Abby Martin. Seriously. We all know you're with her.

ETHAN: It's true, bro.

FINN: Exactly.

REID: And here I thought I was friends with a bunch of dudes not a bunch of women. Why are we talking about my love life…

ETHAN: Because you refuse to admit you have one. With Abby.

FINN: Damn... Ethan comin' in hot with the burn.

REID: Fuck all of you.

REID: But let's just say I was seeing Abby. How do I get her into this "book club"

JACKSON: I'll get Mila to reach out.

FINN: So poker night...

Dinner with a Scottish father and a French mother means a lot of rich and hearty food. Make that dinner *Christmas* dinner and suddenly it's a feast for the senses. Roast turkey with chestnut stuffing, potatoes, vegetables done in an au gratin style, and of course a cheese platter to round it all out pairs perfectly with the wines I stopped to buy at the specialty wine store I always go to in Vancouver. Just as she does every year, Mom has the house looking like it belongs in a magazine. Seriously, it's as if Christmas threw up in here, but somehow in a beautifully elegant way. As I sip the cognac she poured for us all after we finished stuffing our faces with dessert, I wander through the living room, looking at all of the family photos she insists on displaying. My favourite will always be the one of me in my grandfather's arms, holding a spray of grapes. The very same grapes I have been nurturing for the last several months, hoping and praying they'll take root in the very different climate of Vancouver Island. This spring will be the real test, when we see just how strong the shoots are.

The very real pang of nerves, mixed with pride, mixed with sorrow, fills me as it does every time I see this photo. I have a copy hidden in a drawer at home, waiting for the day that La Lune Rouge is producing this wine that connects me to the man I admired and loved so much. The man I miss so much.

"Hello, mon cher. How did I know you would be here," my mother says, coming to kiss my cheek affectionately. "He would be so proud of you."

I turn to face her. "I can't help but wish I had been able to show him what I've done with his grapes. If only I'd tried to come home sooner."

"If you had not spent the time in California building your skills and gaining experience, Pierre would not have offered you this opportunity. You wouldn't have your own winery, producing exquisite wines. You would be a slave to someone else, at their whim for what happens to the grapes. You would not have lived up to your dream."

Her gentle slap to my arm underlies the indignant tone of her voice. Mom never shies away from saying what needs to be said, and in this instance, as in many others, she's right.

"I know. I just hate that I'll never be able to pour him a glass of wine that I have made."

Her eyes soften and she draws me over to the sofa. "Sit, sit down and talk to me. You are very sentimental tonight, my darling son."

I follow her and sink down into the plush, velvet-covered sofa that has lived in this house since I was a child. It's worn in places, and I rub my hand absently over one such spot.

"Now talk to me. Is everything going well with Pierre?"

I swirl the amber liquid in my glass for a moment, thinking of how to respond. I don't want to say too much, because I know my parents will want to help and I'm determined not to take their money. But I've always had a close relationship with my parents, and not letting them in on my worries feels wrong.

"Everything is going well. We're on schedule for a soft opening later this spring. We're simply having a difference of opinions about the tasting room."

My dad chooses that moment to walk in. He sits in a large armchair next to the stone fireplace and turns from me to my mother.

"What are we talking about that has such serious looks on your faces? It's Christmas. Time for joy and happiness."

Mom reaches over and pats his knee, and the loving look she gives him strikes a chord in me. Their fairy-tale marriage set the bar so high for me in terms of love, it almost seems unattainable. But deep inside, hidden in a part of me I don't let show often, I want that. I want a partner, a lover, a wife. Someone by my side, pushing me to be better than I am, yet loving who I am, no matter what.

"Finnigan was just saying he and Pierre have a difference of opinion, mon amour."

I sip my cognac as Dad lifts her hand and presses a kiss to the back of it before turning to me. "About what, son?"

"The tasting room," I admit. "He wants to hire the daughter of a friend of his to design it. She's got some crazy ideas that he loves, but I'm not so sure about it."

"Do you not like the design?"

"No, I do," I answer reluctantly. "It's just that the design seems...extravagant. More so than I had initially envisioned for the space."

Mom quirks a small smile at me. "Is it the design you struggle with, or the cost of the design?"

I let out a wry chuckle. "A mother's intuition never fails you, does it?"

"No mon cher, it does not."

My dad leans forward and rests his elbows on his knees, looking at me. "Son, I know you don't want our help with the money, and I respect that. But that does not mean I won't offer. We want you to feel as confident in your success as we do."

Gratitude fills me. I know I'm damn lucky to have parents like this. "Thanks, Dad. It'll be okay, though. Pierre and I just need to work out the details, and I just have to make sure Ashley doesn't go too crazy with the budget. If I can get her on my side, understanding the need for some restraint, we'll be fine."

"Well, son. You'll catch more bees with honey than with vinegar, if you know what I mean."

"Yeah, Dad. I know what you mean."

I drain my cognac glass, as conversation shifts to the trip to Australia my parents have planned for next fall. But my mind is only half engaged in what they're talking about. The other half is formulating a plan to do just what Dad said.

I'll win Ashley over, professionally, of course.

Personally, I'll keep her at arm's length. That's the only safe distance for a woman who is capable of both tempting me and tormenting me, the way I suspect she is.

Chapter Six

Ashley

Christmas with my dad was exactly what I needed to get my head on straight. He reminded me that my unique style is what makes me so talented as a designer. The passion I have for the kind of spaces I like to design is evident in the work I've already done, and I've got a long list of happy clients singing my praises.

If the work I want to do isn't in downtown Vancouver anymore, then so be it. Maybe it's time for me to look elsewhere. I don't want to leave the city, Lord knows I'll miss the energy, the restaurants, and the shopping, but I can't enjoy any of that if I don't have work.

Now I'm back on Vancouver Island, driving through a snowstorm to get to the winery for a meeting with Pierre and Finn.

I hunch forward, staring out my windshield at the flakes coming down outside. Snow this heavy isn't common for the West Coast, so it always rattles me when it hits. But I've got good tires and Dad made sure I knew how to drive in snow when I was a teenager. Slowly I make my way to La Lune Rouge, thanking the powers that be that the roads are plowed here.

When I arrived on the island yesterday and got settled in the Airbnb I've booked a suite at for the next few months, it was cold outside, but the skies were clear. But things can change quickly, as today's weather proves. When I woke up this morning, my room was cold but heated up quickly once I turned on the gas fireplace. The suite I'm staying in is cute and spacious, the only downside is I have to share a bathroom with the other suite. But since no one else is staying there right now, I have the place to myself.

I let out a long sigh of relief when I finally pull in to park in front of the building that will eventually house the tasting room and wine shop at La Lune Rouge. I don't see any other vehicles, but Pierre made sure I had a key to the space before I left for Christmas, so I let myself inside. Shivering at the cold air, I turn up the thermostat and turn on the lights. Those fluorescent bulbs have got to go, and when I spy the boxes I had shipped over from the mainland, I smile. *Perfect.* But before I can open them to make sure everything arrived intact, the door opens, bringing in a gust of cold air.

"Shit, it's freezing in here."

I turn to see Finn removing his ball cap and brushing snow off of it. "A toque would keep your head warmer, you know," I say, unable to resist the dig. The last thing I need is for him to realize that a guy wearing a backwards ball cap is like catnip for me. There isn't much that I find hotter than that.

He doesn't say anything right away, just looks at me silently. It's unnerving and I shift from one foot to the other, wondering if I should apologize for my snark. But the bite to his response has me rethinking that apology.

"Yeah, but a toque wouldn't turn you on as much as my hat does, now would it?"

A shocked gasp escapes me before I can stop it. "I don't...what...I..." *shitshitshitshitshit*. How the hell did he figure that out?

His low chuckle doesn't help. Neither does the disdain in his voice when he replies. "It's okay, princess. You don't have to say anything. It's obvious."

I close my eyes and try to find some sense of calm before I speak. "Is Pierre on his way?"

If Finn cares that I'm changing the subject, he doesn't let it show. "I don't think he's going to make it. He's stubborn and refuses to put snow tires on his car, so he won't drive in this."

Great. I'm stuck here with mister tall, dark, and scruffy all by myself.

"Alright. Well, I guess we can get started then. You've seen the final design?"

Finn nods but doesn't say a word. For a guy who had some strong opinions last time we spoke, he's strangely silent now.

"Any thoughts? Feedback? Did you review the budget I sent with the design?" I fold my arms in front of me. He has the decency to allow a flash of guilt mar his face.

"No. I didn't want it to ruin my time with my parents."

I huff out a laugh. "God, could you be any more dramatic?" I inhale deeply and exhale out my nose. Why does he have to make this so difficult? "Fine. If you're going to let a few numbers on a piece of paper scare you, I'll have to show you."

I turn away and walk over to where the boxes I had shipped over are placed. So far not much has arrived, and it won't until we've tackled the necessary construction and painting. But these were things I had in storage, waiting for the right project. And the tasting room is that project. Just inside the top of one box holds the papers I'm looking for. I thrust them out to him, and shake my hand when he doesn't immediately take them.

"Take it. They won't bite."

He narrows his eyes at me slightly, and the intensity of his gaze makes me shiver. But he finally unfolds the receipts and invoices and glances down. I watch his face carefully and it doesn't disappoint.

"Wait. This says...no way, that price must be wrong." He glances up at me, his brow furrowed. "I've done my research, princess, I know how much live edge wood tables and blown glass sconces cost."

It's the second time he's called me princess and I turn my head so he doesn't see my grimace. There's no way he could know how much that stings, but I'll be damned if I let him know it gets to me. Instead, I straighten my spine and lift one of the sconces out of the box, carefully unwrapping it from the protective packaging.

"They don't cost nearly as much at estate sales. When I said sustainable purchasing was a cornerstone of my work, I meant it. I don't buy new unless I have to. I've had these pieces in storage for almost a year, waiting for the right space to use them. The tables and the matching bar top are still on the mainland, I need to rent a truck to bring them over. But that's why the dimensions for the bar are so exact. The piece I have for the top is already finished and it's spectacular. When the owner said he was getting rid of it, I couldn't let it go to waste." I'm babbling, I know, but there's a peculiar light in his eyes, and it's getting to me. He's not looking at me with distrust, he's looking at me with admiration. And that's a heady feeling.

"What about the rest of the furnishings? Paint, shelving, glasses. We can't get all of that from estate sales." He sounds curious, not judgmental, and I fight back a smile, I'm so eager to show him what I can do.

"I happen to know a guy. He's a distributor for restaurants for dishes and glassware. When I went home, I got in touch with him and asked him to let me know if he comes across what we're looking for."

"So, that will be new?"

I move my head back and forth, trying to figure out how to explain it. "Sort of. Yes, they'll be new, but...they might not be exactly what you asked for."

It's his turn to arch a brow at me, and I know I'm on the cusp of losing his agreement.

"You would be surprised how often restaurants get close to opening, only to fold under the financial burden." I don't miss the wince he tries to hide, which solidifies my resolve. "Bert has a buyback program where he allows those places to return the products they've ordered from him, but at a discounted price. Which he then passes on to me." I smile triumphantly.

"Why does he do that?"

It's my turn to wince. But now's not the time to shy away from the truth. "Because he's a client of my dad's."

At Finn's scowl, my hackles go up. "Don't look at me like that. I'm not some spoiled brat, some *princess* who lets her daddy solve all her problems. Yes, my dad handles Bert's investments. Yes, that's how I met Bert. But negotiating a deal with him to be able to purchase things for my clients at a reduced cost? That was all me." I place my hands on my hips at his skeptical expression. "I'll have you know, it's not easy as a freelance designer to build connections with vendors, especially not when being cost aware and environmentally aware is so important to me. Okay, fine, I took advantage of a personal connection to someone. So. What. It's the only time I've done it, and I don't regret it. Now if you're ready to stop trying to tell me how to do my job, maybe we can move on. Don't you need to go and squish some grapes or something?"

When I finish my rant, I'm breathing heavily. But Finn isn't looking at me with that critical eye anymore. Now it seems as if he's fighting back a laugh. Maybe that should make me mad, but he's so handsome, even more so when he smiles and that dimple pops out; I can't hide my own grin.

"Squishing grapes, huh? Is that what you think I do?"

I shrug.

"Come on, *Ashley,*" he winks when he says my name and I'd be a liar if I didn't admit it makes my stomach flutter.

"I do a lot more than squish grapes. But even if that was what I did, I can't exactly squish anything now, in the middle of a snowstorm, when the grapes aren't even ready to be squished."

A giggle bubbles out of me. "How many times are you going to say the word *squish*?"

His answering laugh is far more relaxed than I've ever heard him. "I dunno. It's a fun word, though."

We smile at each other, and the earlier tension is gone. I'm not foolish enough to believe it won't come back, we're clearly destined to rub each other the wrong way. But this is nice. Nice enough that I've got the courage to come clean.

"I'll be honest. I don't know the first thing about making wine, but," I pause, and tug my lower lip between my teeth. "I'm really good at drinking it."

Finn's eyes darken and his gaze zeroes in on my mouth.

Oh, damn.

Chapter Seven

Finn

It takes all of my self control not to reach out and pull that lip out from between her teeth and kiss her. Fucking hell, working with Ashley might turn out to be harder than I expected it would be. It's certainly not going to be easy with her looking like all of my fantasies come to life. Then again, all I have to do is remember that she represents an expense to the winery that is entirely unnecessary, and I'm less inclined to cooperate. No matter how sexy she is right now.

"Well. When the weather's better, we can go over to the winery where we're currently using the machines to make our wine and I'll show you how it's done." Fuck, that came out sounding way dirtier than I intended, and I can only hope she doesn't read the innuendo that I didn't mean to say. Granted, in a normal circumstance I would have no problem flirting like that. But that can't happen with Ashley. I can't be that way with her.

"I'd like that." Her soft reply is like a jolt of adrenaline to my dick, which is becoming uncomfortable, trapped in the confines of my jeans.

I feel the smile cross my face at her agreement. And wipe it away quickly. "Cool. Pretty soon we'll move production here, but we'll still have to finish the first stage of blending over there. I'll bottle and age the wine here, though."

Ashley's eyes widen. "First stage of blending? Wow. I really had no idea how much work went into wine." A pretty pink flush comes over her cheeks, giving her an innocent appearance that I wish I didn't like quite so much. "I'm kind of embarrassed that I'm working on a tasting room for a winery, and am completely clueless about winemaking."

"It's okay. Pierre and I will turn you into a pro in no time." Crap. I need to rein it in. I know how eager I get when I start talking about winemaking, no matter who I'm talking to. If there's a person willing to listen to me, I'll go on and on. But I've got to keep it in check around Ashley. There's no point in warming up to her when she's here to do a job and then she'll be gone.

"Perfect."

"Perfect," I echo. We stand there, staring at each other in silence for a second before I realize there's a connection forming between us that I need to steer clear of. "Anyway, I guess we should be going before the weather gets worse." I turn away from her, grateful for my long winter coat that covers the evidence of what she does to me. My body clearly isn't in sync with my mind given this ridiculous reaction to Ashley is purely physical. It's simple biology, an understandable attraction to a beautiful woman. Still, it's a little unnerving.

Ashley walks over to stare out the window where both of our cars are now covered in a blanket of snow. "Oh wow, it's really coming down." She doesn't sound nervous, but I look at her carefully anyway.

"Are you okay to drive in that? I can give you a ride if you need me to."

She turns and the smile she gives me is confident. "Nah, I'm good. I've got snow tires, and my dad made sure I could drive in snow when I was younger. We used to take a yearly trip to Whistler."

I nod and stuff my hands in my pockets. I know we should leave but I'm reluctant to go. There's an undeniable pull between us, in spite of all that she does to drive me crazy. Ashley isn't the evil designer intent on ruining our budget that I previously believed she was. She's got talent, lots of it, and her commitment to cost-effectiveness and environmentally friendly practice is admirable. She's also one hell of an alluring woman, and I need to find a way to work with her without letting my baser desires get in the way.

Easy. No problem.

Right, I don't believe me either.

The drive back to the house I'm renting in town takes way too fucking long thanks to the storm, and I can't help but wonder if Ashley made it back safely to wherever she's staying. I guess I'll have to get her cell number so we can keep in touch about work, but right now I wish I had it so I could check on her. If my concern for her well-being doesn't tell me how far gone I already am on this woman, I don't know what does. I'm not the guy who worries about the women he's dating, mostly because I don't exactly *date*. I meet a woman when I want some company, we enjoy ourselves, and then we go our separate ways.

But Ashley isn't some woman I met at a bar. No she's not. And it's perfectly fine for me to be concerned about her as a co-worker, but nothing more. Still, there's nothing I can do right now since I don't have her number. So I push any unwanted thoughts about her out of my mind as I climb out of my car, pulling the collar of my jacket tight around my neck against the freezing air. I'm going to need to come back out and shovel off my front path and driveway. It's kind of a miracle I managed to get my car in as it is.

But when I eventually get around to the back door that leads to the laundry room where I plan on grabbing some warmer clothes and gloves, it's clear that a snow-covered driveway is the absolute least of my problems.

The roof of the small laundry room that was a poorly built addition to the original house (according to Ethan, the construction expert) has caved in from the weight of the snow that must have piled onto it. Underneath the drifts, I can make out the shape of the washer and dryer, and I can see snow piled up in the hallway that leads to the rest of the house.

This is bad. Really bad.

I quickly turn around and make my way to the front of the house and let myself inside. The furnace is still pumping, so at least it's a little warm in here. Then again, that could be a bad thing if all the snow melts. I look around and don't see any other damage, but I keep my boots on as I walk through the main floor to check things out. Yeah, it's bad. The snow from the laundry room is piling up, big time. Thinking quickly, I jog back out to my car and grab the emergency tarp I keep in there. The toolbox Ethan gave me as a gag gift when I moved in is sitting on the floor in my living room, and I open it for the first time to grab a hammer and some nails. I make quick work of attaching the tarp to the doorframe that leads to the hallway and the destroyed laundry room, hoping that it will stop more snow from drifting in.

When that's done, my heart is racing from adrenaline. This is not exactly what I thought I would be doing tonight. I grab my phone and call my landlord to update them on the situation. Their shock is unmistakable, and they promise to come straight out and take a look.

An hour later, it's getting dark outside and my landlord has gone home after agreeing to refund my rent for the month and apologizing profusely, even though this is mother nature's fault and not theirs. Unfortunately, with this freak storm, there's no telling when they can get someone to fix the roof, which means I need to find somewhere else to stay, and fast.

I stomp upstairs and open my closet door, tossing clothes into a pile on my bed. At least the damage is contained to the laundry room. Still, this is the last goddamn thing I want to be worrying about right now, but thankfully I've got a responsible landlord who will take care of it when they can.

Ethan and his sister Mila own most of the rental properties in town, but this house isn't one of theirs. If it was, I know for a fact one of them would be insisting I stay with them until it's fixed. Hell, I could probably ask them for a place to sleep anyway, but I don't want to. They're both in relatively new relationships, as is Reid, now that he and Abby Martin have hooked up. Having an unexpected houseguest is probably going to cramp their style, and I don't think I want to invade their privacy like that.

Thankfully, Dogwood Cove has a couple of Airbnb's, and when I check online, one of them has a suite available. Shared kitchenette and bathroom, but that doesn't bother me as long as the room has a lock. I won't be there long, and most of my time will be spent out at the winery anyway. I click confirm on my booking, and turn back to packing a bag.

I'm just zipping my duffel bag shut when my phone buzzes with an incoming message from the person who owns the Airbnb. She lets me know the code to unlock the door and get into my suite, sends over a few guidelines, and asks me to please be quiet when I arrive as the other guest is already in their suite. Sure. Fine. As long as I have someplace to sleep where snow isn't *inside* the house, I'm good.

I'm forced to drive at a crawl the entire way to the Airbnb. Fuck, this storm is something else. At least everywhere in Dogwood Cove is relatively close by, so even driving as slowly as I am, I get there in just a few minutes. Something tells me I won't be driving tomorrow, however. Most, if not all of the town, will shut down with this kind of weather, I'm guessing. Hopefully Mila has some extra muffins or something at her house if she's not able to open the bakery.

When I get to the small house where I'll be staying, I grab my bag and lock my car before trudging through the snow to the side door that leads to the suites. As asked, I go in quietly, pausing to hear if any sound is coming from the other suite, but it's silent. When I open the door to my room, I'm pleasantly surprised. It's spacious, with a bed, a desk, a minifridge and a coffee maker. There's a printout on the desk, reiterating the information about the shared kitchen and bathroom, and some etiquette rules. Hopefully I won't be here long, but it's still nice to see the place is well maintained.

Suddenly a wave of exhaustion hits me. It's well after 9 pm, and I haven't even had any dinner. I pull out the takeout boxes I grabbed from my fridge at home on my way out the door. I could go and use the microwave, but honestly, I'm too fucking tired. Cold Chinese food it is. Along with the box of lo mein, I pull out the bottle of sauvignon blanc I snagged from home. Thank fuck it's one of those new style bottles with a screw cap, not a cork. The old-timer winemakers might frown on caps, but right now I'm grateful for it. I don't even bother looking for a glass, just take a long sip from the bottle like the classy sommelier I am.

Good wine makes everything better.

Of course, my fucking phone rings when I have a mouthful of noodles, but when I see it's just Ethan, I answer and give him a mumbled, "Hey."

"Dude, why did your landlady just call and ask me to come over tomorrow to give her a quote on repairing your fucking roof?"

I swallow and roll my eyes at Ethan's concern. "You sound like my mom. It's fine, man." No it's not, that's the wine talking.

"How is it fine? Where are you staying? You can always come here, you know." I can hear Ethan's brain at work, trying to come up with a solution. That's just who he is, always the guy wanting to help everyone else.

"I'm already settled at an Airbnb. Seriously, don't worry. I can stay here until things get figured out with the house." I take another swallow of wine from the bottle, letting the cool, crisp liquid pool in my mouth so I can truly savour the taste. Citrus notes, a hint of green apple, and a slight spicy afternote hit my palate. It's not great wine, but it's not bad. I can do better. But it's doing the trick for now.

"You're sure?" Ethan says.

"Yes. I'm sure. I appreciate the concern, but it's all good. I don't need to invade your little love nest."

"Oh, fuck off, man," he grumbles, but I can hear Summer's cheerful voice in the background saying, "He's not wrong, babe."

I chuckle. "Yeah. See? Now stop worrying like an old lady, and let me get back to my dinner."

"Okay. Fine. I'll go have *sex* with my *fiancée* in my *love nest* then."

"Enjoy, asshole."

I drop my phone back down on my bed with a smile on my face. I appreciate Ethan's concern, and it means a lot that he reached out. But that's also just the kind of guy he is, always wanting to take care of people and help however he can. Honestly, the winery being located in Dogwood Cove is what my mom likes to call serendipity. Bringing me back to Canada, and back in touch with my good friends.

Jesus Christ, I'm getting sentimental. I eye the bottle of wine. It's only half full, not nearly enough to blunt these weird emotions I'm not used to feeling. But it's all I have for now, at least until I can get back home and raid my wine rack some more. Maybe grab the bottle of whiskey I keep above the fridge as well.

Half an hour later my food is gone, the bottle is empty, and it's all I can do to strip off my clothes and climb into the bed and let sleep overtake my exhausted body.

Chapter Eight

Ashley

I slept like a rock last night. Whether it was from the orgasm I gave myself when I came home, still buzzing from a Finn-induced high, or simply being tired from the background stress of the snowstorm, I don't know. Either way, I'm actually feeling pretty good today. And when I look outside, there's a pleasant surprise. The snow has stopped, but everything is coated in a thick layer of the white stuff. The sun is shining, making my eyes water against the bright light beaming back at me. But it certainly is beautiful.

There's no one around to see me grinning and dancing around my room like a goof. Snow days always made me happy as a kid; no school, nothing to do except play with my friends. It's different as an adult, less time to play and all that, but the joy is still there inside of me, just seeing the winter wonderland outside. It's such a rare occurrence here on the coast, it never fails to instill the same sense of wonder.

I peel off my pajamas and wrap my short, silk robe around my waist instead before picking up my towel and wash bag. A hot shower, a cup of coffee, and then I'll make a plan for the day.

Opening the music app on my phone, I press play on one of my favourite playlists to get going in the morning. Pretty soon the upbeat tones and sultry voice of Nash Parker, country music sensation and all-around sexy man has me dancing and singing along as I go down the short hall to the bathroom.

"Now all I see is you..." I croon with my eyes closed and push open the bathroom door only to be met with a wall of steam.

"What the fuck?" A deep, masculine, *familiar* voice shocks the crap out of me.

My eyes fly open.

Finn. Naked. Shower. Ohmygod.

"Ashley? What are you doing? Close the damn door, woman!" He roars at me, but I'm frozen, my eyes tracking the water droplets trailing down his naked torso, just barely obscured by the clear glass door of the shower. There's a smattering of hair on his chest, just enough to be manly without being a bear, and my hand comes up to check for drool on my face.

"Do you mind, princess?"

My gaze snaps up to his face and the spell is broken. He's not even trying to hide from me, and I feel the intensity of his stare judging me.

"I...sorry. I didn't know you...sorry. Oh. Wow. Okay. Bye." I step back and slam the door closed, hearing a low groan followed by a "fucking hell" come from the room I just left. My feet run back to the safety of my bedroom where I fling myself down on the bed face first and let out a muffled scream of my own.

Seriously. Did that just happen? Did I really just walk in on Finn, naked in the shower, and then stand there like a freaking pervert?

Yep. I did. And good Lord, I'm fairly certain that never, in my entire adult life, have I seen a sight that turned me on as much as I am right now. If I thought I was buzzing after our casual, not even flirty, conversation last night, it's nothing compared to what I'm feeling between my legs in this moment. Those muscles, his tattoos that until now have been hidden under long sleeves, the perfect little treasure trail of hair that led down to...well, you know. And *that* was just...perfection.

I let my eyes flutter closed, and instantly my imagination starts thinking of how differently things could have gone this morning. Like Finn inviting me to join him. Or maybe he comes to my room after his shower and...

Wait a minute, why is he here?

My eyes fly open and I bolt upright, ready to storm back down the hall and demand an explanation. But then there's a knock at my door that makes my breath catch.

"The roads are plowed, so we should be fine to head to the winery. Do you want to ride together?" His voice sounds rough, like he doesn't really want to offer, but he wants to be polite. This man is so confusing.

"No, I'll drive myself. Are you going to explain why I found you showering at my Airbnb?" I fold my arms across my chest, glaring at the door that separates us.

"Funny, I didn't realize you owned the place. Your voice sounded pretty different on the phone last night, *Elaine,*" comes his retort.

I huff out a breath of exasperation. "You know what I meant."

"My roof caved in from the snow, okay princess? I'll stay out of your way if you stay out of the bathroom when I'm naked. Deal?"

My mouth falls open like a guppy. He did *not* just say that. I go to reply, but then I hear the distinct sound of footsteps going down the hall and the door across the way opening and closing firmly.

This conversation is over, apparently.

This is bad. Like so, so, so bad. I'm not ashamed of my sexual nature, I enjoy a good orgasm as much as the next woman. But this? This next-level fantasizing about a man I absolutely cannot touch? A man I have to not only *work* with but now also *live* with for the foreseeable future? This is not good.

I take my time getting ready, and try to ignore how good the bathroom smells with the aroma of Finn's body wash lingering in the air. When I get outside, my car is cleared of snow.

That's surprisingly nice for a guy who barks at me more than anything.

As Finn said, the roads are plowed, making my short drive to The Nutty Muffin easy, if slow. Right on cue, my stomach growls, and finally, thoughts of Finn are replaced with thoughts of pastries and coffee.

"Hey! Designer girl is back!"

Mila's cheerful greeting rises above the chatter of the busy café. I give her a wave and make my way to the back of the short line, taking the chance to peruse the chalk board outlining what's available today. I don't realize anyone is beside me until I hear her voice again, only this time, it's a lot closer.

"Care to tell me why my buddy Finn was in here not so long ago and seemed a little distracted? When I asked him about it, he just grumbled something about Ashley and a shower. I've never seen the guy with such a grouchy expression on his face."

"Wait, he said *what?*" At the sound of Serena's voice, I trip over my own feet. "Oh sorry, girl. Didn't mean to surprise you. Oh, it's you! Ferry girl!"

My head darts back and forth between the two women as I try to process what's going on. Okay, logically it makes sense. They're friends. Of course, if I'm going to run into Serena, it would be here. But it just seems like so long ago that she and I met on the ferry.

"Hi. I, ah, don't really know what to say," I start lamely. The line moves forward, but instead of going back to work, Mila loops her arm with mine and leans in close.

"Truthfully, I think it's awesome. Finn McNeil needed someone to knock him off kilter and you've done just that. Bravo."

"Yup. And I can't even be mad that you've only been here a short while and you've already taken one of our very few eligible men off the market, because one — eww, it's Finn, and he's like a brother. And two, you're cool, so yay!"

My head is officially spinning, but one thing is certain. I need to clear up a misunderstanding before word gets back to the man in question. "We aren't together. Except for working together, I guess," I say quickly.

Mila lets out a small sound of disappointment. "Then what's the deal with the shower?"

Before I can answer, Serena's pointing at my cheeks. "Ooh, she's blushing! *Something* happened, that's for sure."

"I saw him naked." The words come out louder than I expected. Oh God, did it suddenly get quiet in here?

A beat later, the sounds of the café return, and I blow the air out of my mouth.

"Now that sounds like a story."

"A story that needs alcohol to accompany it." Serena takes my other arm. "Assuming you drink, that is. Not that it matters, we don't care."

"Are you thinking what I'm thinking?"

"That she should come to Hastings with everyone? Heck yes, she should. Ashley, you're coming. Perfect chance to meet everybody. Text me where you're staying and I'll pick you up."

It's like watching a game of table tennis the way my head is going back and forth while the two women talk, and apparently make plans for me.

"Oh wait, I need your number."

Serena's got her phone open and is staring at me expectantly, so I rattle it off automatically. A few seconds later my phone vibrates.

"Perfect. That's me. Yay! I'm so excited!" Serena blows an air kiss in our direction, then spins around in a pirouette. "Alright, time to go teach my little angels how to be butterflies. Bye, ladies!"

"She's always like that," Mila says affectionately, watching her friend leave.

"A whirlwind?" I ask, then wince, hoping she doesn't take that the wrong way. The giggle she makes in return is a relief.

"That's the perfect description. Gotta love her."

We've made it to the front of the line, so Mila goes behind the counter. "Alright, what can I get you today?"

"A cinnamon bun please, and a large hazelnut latte."

"You got it, girl."

Moments later, Mila hands me my order. "I hope you really do come and hang out with us tomorrow. It would be nice to get to know you."

The genuine tone in her voice, paired with the smile she gives me, makes me feel all warm inside. Man, I wish I had people like this back home.

"I'd love to come, thank you."

"Great! Text Serena. Okay, I gotta go, those muffins aren't going to bake themselves."

With one last cheerful wave, Mila bustles into the back of the café, and I make my way to my car.

There's definitely something to be said for small towns. Whatever it is, the people here are so kind and welcoming.

If only there was a good sushi restaurant, I might be tempted to stay.

Chapter Nine

I've called every single motel and hotel, every Airbnb that I can find within a half-hour of the winery in an attempt to find somewhere else to stay. Somewhere that I won't run the risk of my ultimate temptation seeing my naked ass.

Unfortunately, there's a convention on the island or something, and every place is full. Which is rare, unheard of even, according to Ethan. He again offered for me to stay with him and Summer, and I'm almost at that point. Almost.

Between getting up early to hit the gym, and staying at the winery as late as possible, I've managed to avoid seeing Ashley at the house. I hear her and I smell her, or at least I hear her walking around. I smell her shampoo, or soap, or whatever girly product she uses that smells like citrus and fucking sunshine. But at least I haven't had to look at her.

I've been showering at the gym, and the lack of privacy both there and at the Airbnb means it's been over a week since I was able to relieve the tension building in me with every passing moment I have to spend around her. She's driving me crazy, and there's not a goddamn thing I can do about it.

"Finn. I'm glad I caught you today." I glance up from the notes I'm studying on how I plan to blend the chardonnay grape juice arriving soon. Pierre's walking toward me with a focused look on his face.

"Ashley says she will have the flooring samples next week, and the bar is being installed soon. Have you finalized the location for the fridges and sinks behind the tasting counter?"

"Yes." I nod. It's an easy decision; I'm copying my favourite layout from a winery in Napa. A large circle shape that allows for good flow and spacing between customers, as well as plenty of room for staff behind. An overhead rack for glasses, pendant lighting, stools, and a foot rail will round out the focal point of the tasting room. Ashley was disappointed we wouldn't be using her live edge wood for the bar, but even she had to agree the circular design was better. And instead, the live edge will go as the main focal point in the shop area, along one wall that has large windows overlooking the land where our grapes will soon grow.

"Things are going well with her, non?"

My head whips around to stare at Pierre.

"I mean, yeah. I think so, why?"

He shrugs in that relaxed, laissez-faire way only the French can. "She is doing a good job. That is all."

I internally heave a sigh of relief. "Right. Yeah, she is."

"And she tells me she is making friends with your friends. Do you think she is happy?"

"Why the questions, Pierre?"

"Her father, he worries. He asks me how she is."

I consider how to answer without letting on about any of the buried sexual tension I'm fighting.

"I've heard that she's spending time with my friends' girl-friends, yes."

"Good. Good. Ashley, she and her father are special to me. We must treat her well," Pierre says, drumming his fingers on the table where I'm working. He's still staring at me, a thoughtful expression on his face, and I'm having a hard time not showing any reaction that might give something away.

"C'est bon. I will go now, I am meeting with the mayor about a permitting issue. He is one of your friends, is he not?"

"Yes, Ethan and I went to university together," I answer.

"Excellent, then hopefully there will be no delay. We will meet again when Ashley has the samples."

With one final drum of his fingers, Pierre leaves. Me, I stay standing where I am with only one thought clear in my mind.

Ashley Elliott is off limits.

"I'm sorry, man, I wish I had better news, but it's just not possible to finish any faster."

Ethan and I are standing in the backyard of my rental house, looking at the mess left behind when the snow melted. Water drips off the corner where the roof used to connect to the laundry room addition, adding to a mud puddle at our feet.

"Fucking hell, Ethan." I run my hands through my hair in frustration. "I'd live in the house anyway if it weren't so goddamn cold."

"It's only cold because you've still got so much California blood running through your veins."

My eyes lift in a massive eyeroll at his pathetic attempt at teasing me. "Whatever." Together we turn and head back to the front of the house.

"Is it really so bad staying at the Airbnb with Ashley?" Ethan shoots me a sly glance. "I saw her come into the bakery the other day. She's hot."

I glare at him. "Dude. You're engaged."

Ethan just laughs. "And *that* is all the answer I need." Somehow the asshole dodges the fist I throw at his shoulder and walks back to his truck still chuckling. "See you later at Hastings!"

Shaking my head, I go inside the freezing house. I was lying when I said I would live here anyway, it's damp and cold, and I know Ethan isn't joking when he says it's going to take time to fix everything. When the laundry room roof collapsed, it also damaged something on the main part of the house. I don't understand it exactly, but I trust Ethan.

Taking the stairs two at a time, I go back to my bedroom and grab some more clothes to take to the Airbnb. Then back down to the kitchen, where I raid my wine rack for a few bottles of my personal favourites. Then, essentials in hand, I lock up the front door — pointless as that feels when the back of the house is wide open to the world — and I make the short drive back to where I'm forced to stay for the foreseeable future. Ashley's car is parked outside, but when I step inside, I see the door to her room is shut. Perfect. I should be able to get in and get out without running into her. Once I've dropped everything off in my room, I grab my gym bag and leave again. Is it childish to be avoiding her like this? Probably. Do I care? Not at all. If keeping my distance is the only way to avoid temptation, then that's what I'll do.

Two hours later, after a workout and showering at the gym, I open the door to Hastings Bar. We haven't all gathered together since the live nativity before Christmas, so I'm looking forward to having a couple of beers and relaxing with my friends. But that's short-lived when I see Ashley sitting between Paige and Summer. I make my way to the other end and drop down into a seat beside Reid. "What's she doing here," I mutter under my breath, trying not to turn in her direction.

"Who, Ashley? Mila invited her." Reid slaps me on the back and pushes a sleeve of beer my way. "Drink up, my friend. It's Friday night, and we finally all managed to make our schedules line up to hang out."

Right. He has no idea why I wish Ashley wasn't here. Hell, no one does. I'm sure Mila and Ethan suspect it, but I guess the gossip hasn't made it around the group yet. I take a drink from my beer and chance a quick look toward Ashley, only to see her eyes focused on me. Shit. I turn away and focus on whatever Reid and Jackson are talking about.

"I'm telling you, according to Matt, this guy down in Sonoma is the only person on the coast with the part. He's freaking out over how to get it. Hey, Finn, when you were down in California did you ever head to Sonoma?"

I arch my eyebrow at Reid's ridiculous question. "Seeing as Napa and Sonoma are not that far apart, yeah, I did. A lot."

Reid ignores my barb at his lack of understanding of California geography. "Got any suggestions on where to stay down there? One of the teachers needs some specialty piece for his motorcycle, and this guy Lukas Donovan has a shop in Sonoma; apparently, his is the only place on the West Coast that has it. He's thinking of driving down on spring break."

We talk for a while, and I give him a few suggestions for his co-worker. There are definitely parts of California I miss, but this — being back with my friends and closer to my family — is what it's all about. Opening my own winery, even if we won't have many estate wines that we can truly call our own, is a dream come true.

Two sleeves of beer later I'm ready to head home. It's been a long day and an even longer week. My bed is calling, and if going home from a bar before midnight is considered lame, well, sign me up.

"Finn, my buddy, my pal, my favourite wine guy ever." Mila drapes her arms over my shoulders. "You haven't had more than a couple beers, have you?"

I shift in my seat to look at her. "Of course not."

"Great! So you can drive Ashley back to the Airbnb. She's had a little, tiny, teeny bit more." Mila giggles and it's clear all of the girls might have enjoyed a few too many drinks.

"Be honest, Mills. You're all drunk," Ethan says, standing up and wrapping his arm around Summer's waist. She leans into him and sighs.

"Yep, we are, lumberjack."

My eyes find Ashley, who sure enough is swaying in her seat, smiling at something Paige just said. She seems happy, and it looks like she's been a part of our group for a lot longer than a few weeks.

"You good to get her home?" Ethan's voice brings me back.

"Yeah. It's fine," I answer gruffly. Standing up, I chuck a few bills into the middle to cover my part of the tab, then make my way down to where Ashley is sitting.

"Come on, princess. Time to go."

"Ooh, are you my chariot?" She looks up at me with those wide eyes, lined with something that gives her an extra layer of sexy tonight. Not that she needs it. I'd have to be blind not to be attracted to her physically. That's the fucking problem. Without even trying, this woman gets under my skin.

"Sure. Whatever. Just don't expect a white knight. Let's go."

I know I'm being a lot less charming than I normally am around women, or hell, around anyone. But I can't let her get to me. I also can't be that much of an ass, my mama would smack me if I was, so I hold her jacket out and help her get it on.

"Thank you," she murmurs. We say goodbye to everyone else, and walk out to my car together. The night is cold, but thankfully dry. Ashley seems sober all of a sudden, as if the impact of us leaving the bar together isn't lost on her, either. But then she stumbles in the parking lot and lets out a loud curse before clapping her hand over her mouth and giggling.

"Pretend that didn't happen, okay, mister tall, dark, and scruffy?" she says in a sing-song voice before smacking her head with her hand again. "Oh my God. And that."

"Mister tall, dark, and what?" I say, feeling a smile creep across my face as I reach a hand out to steady her. She's adorable, stumbling around like a baby deer just learning to walk or something.

"Nothing. I said nothing." She mimes zipping her mouth shut. "You heard nothing. Got it?"

Shaking my head, I decide to let it go. Not like I could let things go anywhere, even if flirtatious Ashley is proving to be almost more than I can handle. "Right. Nothing."

We reach my car, and when I walk to the passenger side and open the door for her, Ashley stares at me for a second before smiling and placing her hands on her chest. "My hero." She giggles as she climbs in, and I close my eyes in exasperation. She's not making this easy. When I get in and turn the car on, her head lolls to the side so she's facing me with a happy grin.

"You're nothing like my ex, you know? He wouldn't open doors for me." She snorts indelicately. Apparently, drunk Ashley is a chatty Ashley. I shift in my seat and start to pull out of the parking spot, hoping she'll stop oversharing.

No such luck.

"I guess I should have known he'd cheat on me."

Wait. What?

"I just can't believe he found another woman willing to fuck him. He *suuucked* in bed. Like seriously sucked, and not in the good way." Ashley dissolves into giggles and rolls her head to face out the window. She's quiet for a moment, and when she starts to talk again, the laughter is gone from her voice. Funny how I sort of miss it. "I always wanted a boyfriend who would open doors for me. Seems so simple, but it means so much. Thanks for giving me that experience at least once."

I'm rendered speechless. Truly, where the fuck do I even start with the shitload of confessions she just dumped in my lap. Thankfully, she takes my silence as a cue to stop talking and the rest of the drive home is devoid of conversation. I probably shouldn't feel so affected by what she told me, but the thought of some asshole cheating on her, hurting her, is enough to make me tighten my grip on the steering wheel to avoid touching her.

When we get back to the Airbnb, she climbs out on her own before I can even get around to open the door. Fine, I won't try to be polite. But when she starts rummaging through her purse, searching for keys, I gently shift in front of her and unlock the door myself. We head down the short hall to the bedrooms in silence.

"Thanks for the ride," she says quietly at her door.

"No problem. I can take you back to get your car tomorrow if you want."

She looks up and shakes her head, then fuck me if she doesn't bite her lip again. "That's okay, I'll walk. Something tells me the fresh air might be a good idea tomorrow." A slight grimace covers her face just before she yawns widely. "Okay, I'm pooped. G'night, Finn."

She opens her door, and like the obsessed moron I am, I stand there watching as she walks in, kicking off her heels in the process, and drops down face first onto her bed, letting out an adorable groan. "Thanks for the ride, Finn," she mumbles into her blanket. Seconds later, faster than I would have expected, seeing as she's fully dressed, quiet snores reach my ears. If I hadn't seen her whole body relax into the bed, I'd wonder if she's faking it. But I'm pretty sure she isn't, so I give in to temptation and watch her for a second, imagining if I was climbing into bed beside her. I'd slowly undress her, tuck her in against my body, and let those cute sounds she's making lull me to sleep.

Fuck. Who the hell am I right now, talking about falling asleep to a woman's snores? Good Lord.

Turning around, I go to my room and grab a couple things before making my way back down the hall. She's managed to curl up on her side, her hands tucked under her face. I quickly cover her with the blanket at the foot of the bed, and leave the things I brought with me on her bedside table before quietly turning off her light and shutting her door.

Then like the sad piece of shit I am, I go to the bathroom, lock the door, and turn on a very, very cold shower.

Chapter Ten

Why am I in bed fully dressed?

And why is my hair stuck to my face?

Two questions I haven't had to ask myself in a very long time. I slowly blink my eyes open with a groan when the pounding in my head registers with my fuzzy brain. My mouth is as dry as the Sahara, and the light streaming in through my open drapes is making me angry.

Note to self, I no longer have the tolerance for tequila that I used to have. Memories of last night come back to me. It was fun hanging out with everyone. They're a great group. And it was good to learn who's who. Summer apparently grew up here, but moved away for a long time. Now she's back and running a beachfront resort. Oh, and she's engaged to Mila's brother Ethan, who's the mayor of the whole darn town. Mila's boyfriend Jackson is a newcomer like me, he's the local veterinarian and they bonded over Mila's dog Milo. Not going to lie, when she told me her dog's name, I stared at her blankly for a moment until she laughed and said she knew how ridiculous it sounded, but she loved it. Abby and Reid showed up after me; he's the school principal and she's the mother of one of his students. Their relationship is pretty new, apparently, but they seem sweet together. The only other person I didn't know was Paige. She's quiet, serious, but really interesting to talk to. And I promised her I'd come to check out her book store, Pages, soon.

When Serena ordered tequila shots, I tried to say no, but she was frustrated with one of her dance moms and insisted we drink. The problem was, with every shot, we had to say something that pissed us off. I'm pretty sure I mentioned Tyson sticking his dick where it didn't belong on shot number two, which then led to even more drinking.

I vaguely remember teasing Finn about being my chariot, when in reality I should be grateful he made sure I got back here safely. Surprising, seeing as he's made it very clear that he's been trying to avoid me this past week. But then again, maybe not. Mila said he's a good guy, and when he doesn't know I'm looking, I watch how he interacts with other people. He's polite, friendly, funny even. Not the distant, cool professional he is around me.

I make my way to sit up, and it's then I realize there's a blanket on top of me. That wouldn't be weird, except it's a blanket I never use, a quilt my grandmother made for me. Huh. Okay, guess drunk Ashley grabbed that one for some reason. Turning my head slowly so that I don't make the headache any worse, I reach for the glass of water that's usually on my bedside table, only to see another surprise. A bottle of orange juice and a bottle of Tylenol are sitting there.

Finn.

More memories come back. Of him opening my door, helping me into the car, catching me when I stumbled. He was kind, sweet even. And now, seeing how he took care of me with the blanket and the juice and everything, well, let's just say he's making it pretty difficult to remember he wants nothing to do with me outside of work.

All I've got to do today is drive to the nearby city of Westport to pick up some things for the tasting room, so after I pop a couple of Tylenol and drink the bottle of juice, I take off my bra and jeans. That's as much as I can be bothered with right now. I drink some water and settle back down under the covers of my bed. In that half awake, half asleep state, I drowse, letting my mind empty and settle. Some time later, I hear the sound of a door opening and closing, and quiet footsteps down the hall that stop outside my door. Freezing, I wait to see what Finn will do. Obviously, my bedroom door isn't locked, since he clearly was in here after I passed out last night to play hangover fairy. After a second of silence, the footsteps continue and I hear the outer door open and close.

Grabbing the pillow beside me, I cover my face and let out a muffled scream.

That man is beyond frustrating.

Eventually, I drag my sorry butt out of bed, and head to the bathroom. Turning the shower on as hot as I can handle, I run a brush through my tangled hair before twisting it up into a knot on the top of my head. I don't have the energy to wash it right now. Stepping into the steaming spray, I let the warmth of the water soothe my ridiculous hangover. I'm too old for this crap.

Who knows how long later, I reluctantly step out of the shower and dry off, then head back to my bedroom to get dressed. Fleetingly, I wonder if Finn came home and if I'll run into him with nothing more than a towel wrapped around my body, a little reflection on our last nearly naked interaction, but no such luck. Part of me wants the opportunity to tease him like that, the other part can't help but be a little nervous of rejection, given the way he acts around me. Or, should I say the way he *has been* acting around me. Maybe things are changing now.

Or maybe he was just being nice to a drunk idiot. Yeah, that's more likely.

Once I'm dressed, I decide against walking to my car. It's too damn cold out there. Thankfully, Dogwood Cove has a couple of Uber drivers, and pretty soon one of them picks me up and drops me off at Hastings. I scrape off the frost that built up on the windshield and get in. Rubbing my hands together against the chill, I wait for the engine to warm up a bit before driving away. First stop, The Nutty Muffin. Mila's got me addicted to her baking, and I might grab a sandwich from the café side to have later for lunch.

My car is just starting to warm up by the time I reach the bakery. I head inside quickly, eager for that first sip of hot coffee to warm me up from the inside. I don't see Mila, but she's probably in the back. A quick scan of the tables doesn't reveal anyone else I recognize, but a couple friendly faces smile, and I smile back.

The line moves quickly, thanks to Mila's efficient staff, and when it's my turn, I order my coffee, muffin, and a sandwich. They let me pay for it all at once, and as soon as I've got my coffee and muffin, I wander through the opened up wall to the café side. The vibe here is different, although the walls are the same warm colour to show the continuity from bakery to café. The café has more tables and less oversized comfy chairs. And the lighting is slightly darker, with more exposed beams and a rustic vibe instead of the cozy bakery next door. They flow well, and once again I'm impressed by Mila's talent at designing the spaces herself.

"Hi, welcome to Camille's. Are you Ashley?" The peppy girl behind the counter greets me with a warm smile.

"Yep, that's me."

She hands me a paper bag. "There you go, one turkey and veggie wrap. Enjoy!"

I give her a smile of thanks and turn to go.

"Ashley!"

At Mila's voice, I turn back around to see her walking out from the back kitchen.

"Sorry. Didn't know you were here until I heard Leanne say your name." Mila walks over and gives me a swift hug. "Please tell me you're hurting today, so I don't feel like the only lame one."

The grimace on my face answers her question.

"Oh, thank God."

"Yeah, no offense to Serena, but that's the last time I do tequila shots with her."

Mila laughs and shakes her head. "She's something else. Won't drink caffeine but mainlines sugar like a champ and can handle booze better than any of us."

I look at her, aghast at what she just said. "She doesn't drink caffeine? How does she survive?"

"I know, I know. It's insane." Mila shakes her head. "Caffeine is life."

I nod and raise my coffee cup. "Amen, sister."

"Anyway, I gotta run," Mila tilts her head over to the bakery. "I'll see you soon, okay? Don't forget book club at my place next week. Paige can hook you up with a copy."

"Yup. See you," I reply. "And thanks for the breakfast!"

"It's what I do! I feed people," she says cheerfully over her shoulder as she makes her way back to the bakery. I turn and head outside into the cold morning and get back into my car, turning it on and taking another sip of coffee. Once I've loaded directions to the first location I'm headed to, I turn on the radio, smiling when my favourite song comes on. Volume up, heater on high, and coffee in hand, I head out, hangover almost forgotten.

Westport is a nice enough city, smaller than Vancouver, but definitely bigger than Dogwood Cove. It's got all the big stores, some restaurants that seem intriguing, and a spa that I definitely want to come back and visit.

Two hours later, I'm leaving the antique store where I managed to negotiate an incredible deal on some vintage art prints for the walls of the wine store, when I hear a voice call my name.

"Ashley Elliott, my God, it is you!"

"Tom Coffman?" I cry out in surprise as he wraps me in a hug.

Tom and I had been such close friends all through design school. We partnered on a lot of projects, even though our design preferences were completely different. Many nights were spent drinking cheap wine and putting the finishing touches on assignments and projects. But after finishing our degrees, we lost touch. Last I heard, he had gone back east to Toronto.

"What the hell are you doing over here, baby girl? I thought you were taking the city by storm?" Tom holds me at arm's length and runs his observant, fashion-forward eyes over me. "Still rocking that boho-chic vibe, I see. Mmm hmm." He turns me from side to side. "Looking good, honey."

I pull him back in for another hug. "It is so good to see you, Tom. And I could ask you the same question, what happened to Toronto?"

"Well...love happened." He drags out that first word, giving me a sly smile, then flips his left hand up to show me a simple band on his ring finger. "I got married!"

"Oh, Tom! Congratulations." I smile, taking his hand in mine. "Tell me everything."

Tom wraps my arm in his and we walk down the sidewalk together. "His name is Leo, he's a freaking doctor, and we moved to Westport a year ago. Now what the hell are you doing here, baby girl?"

"Okay, hang on, a doctor? You married a hot doctor?" I slap him teasingly on the arm. "You found your Doctor McDreamy!" Tom and I had bonded over our obsession with *Grey's Anatomy*, binge watching many episodes during school.

"I sure did. And he is McDreamy and McSteamy, all mixed up in one hunk of handsome."

We come to a stop beside a sushi restaurant and right on cue, my stomach rumbles.

"I'm taking you to lunch," Tom declares.

"I would kill for a salmon roll," I admit, and we head inside.

Over lunch, we catch up on the last few years that we've been apart. Tom admits he's followed my career in Vancouver and commiserates with me on the downturn of the market over there. Design styles are fickle and can change on a whim. We discuss my ideas for the winery, and Tom agrees to come and check it out sometime.

Pretty soon, we're full of sushi and green tea, but we linger over the table chatting. When Tom tells me that he and Doctor McDreamy are looking to adopt a baby, the expression of pure adoration on his face makes me smile.

"You'll be such a great dad," I say, reaching over to cover his hand on the table. He squeezes mine in return.

"Thanks, boo. We just have to figure out what we'll do about work. Leo's so busy with his practice, and my company is insane right now with clients. I just hired an assistant, but it's going to be way too much to handle with a baby in the mix." Tom narrows his eyes at me. "You know, life on the island is pretty amazing. What's a guy gotta do to convince his favourite design bestie to join forces with him?"

If my jaw could hit the floor, it would. "You're offering me a job?"

Tom waves his hand in the air dismissively. "Oh no, honey, I'm offering you a partnership. We always said we wanted to work together, didn't we? And unless you've somehow turned into a total bag in the last few years, I think we'd have a ton of fun. I need the help, and we could offer so much more if we combined forces. Your bohemian vibe, my clean lines, we've got every style covered. And then when I get my baby, I can slow down a bit because I'll have someone I trust in charge. You'd be the answer to my prayers."

I'm speechless. I thought finding a decent sushi place close to Dogwood Cove was a miracle, but this...this is something else.

This could be the answer to all of my problems.

Except, am I ready to leave my Dad, leave the city, leave everything I've ever known? It's not like it's that far away, but still. I would be giving up my own business, which granted, isn't doing so well right now. But still — it's mine. Moving away from my Dad is a tough pill to swallow. My mom died from cancer when I was two, so it's been just the two of us ever since. I've never lived farther than an hour from my childhood home in west Vancouver. Being a ferry ride away feels big, even if it really isn't.

"Can I think about it? I'm honoured, Tom, really. But it's a big decision."

His eyes soften. "Of course, Ash. I'm not trying to pressure you at all. But look, while you're here, you have to come over for dinner with me and Leo."

"I'd love that."

Eventually we pay the bill and head our separate ways. And the entire drive back to Dogwood Cove, I can't help but imagine staying here, making a new life in this small town with all these people I'm starting to love.

And Finn.

When I stop at the winery to drop off the samples I picked up, the man in question is walking around the corner of the tasting room building just as I pull up. He stuffs his hands in the pockets of his jacket and shifts from one foot to the other.

I get out of my car and give him a small wave. "Hi."

"Hey," he says gruffly. "How are you feeling?"

"Fine." God, why is this so awkward? "Thank you for last night." *Shit, that sounds worse.* "I mean for driving me home and the juice and...yeah."

"It's fine." His answers are just as stilted as mine, and if anything, it seems like it pains him to be polite right now. Lord, this man confuses me.

"Right. Well, still, I appreciate it."

He gives me a crisp nod, then walks away without another word.

Alrighty then. Thoughtful Finn is gone, scowly Finn is back.

Chapter Eleven

Finn

"It'll be fun. And probably the only way a city boy like you will ever get to wield an axe."

I glare at Ethan over the top of my treadmill as I slow down from my sprint.

"Thanks, asshole." He steps onto the machine beside me and matches my pace. We're at the gym together, which is rare seeing as Ethan's more into outdoor activities than the gym. But the weather sucks right now, typical January, wet and cold. So he decided to join me this morning. Of course, he was late, and came in with a stupid grin on his face that made it perfectly clear *why* he was late. Perk of a solid relationship, I guess. Morning blowjobs on demand.

I'm in a bad mood. The last thing I want to do is hang out with one of the happy couples. It's been a few days since I drove Ashley home from the bar, and I can't stop thinking about her. It was too much, seeing her all soft and relaxed in her bed that night. It was way too tempting. I know I have to dig in and hold my ground, keep my distance. I need to remember she's here to do a job and that's all. She's not staying, and while that might normally be a good thing, the problem with Ashley is that I'm starting to see she's the kind of woman I would want for more than just a night or two.

I can't pinpoint exactly when that feeling first hit me. Was it watching her with my friends and seeing how easily she integrates into our group? Was it listening to her hum her favourite songs under her breath while she works? Or was it that fire I saw in her eyes way back on the morning when she saw me naked in the shower. I don't know when, but at some point, I stopped seeing Ashley as just a sexy woman I wouldn't mind getting into bed with, and started seeing her as an incredibly talented, smart, funny, and kind woman who I wish I had met under different circumstances.

"So you'll come?"

I tune back in to whatever Ethan's been saying. Summer and Mila apparently planned a double date at some axe throwing place down in Victoria, but Jackson's stuck with a work emergency, so Ethan invited me instead.

"So it'll be me and Mila against you and Summer? That doesn't seem fair," I reply.

Ethan's steps falter slightly. "Ah, yeah, not Mila. Umm, Summer said you should bring Ashley."

I step off to the side edges of my treadmill and stare at my friend. "What are you guys up to?"

He holds his hands up, and shoots me an apologetic look. "Nothing, I swear. I don't know why you're being weird about her, she seems like an awesome girl, but that's not my business. Summer just figured you guys made sense, seeing as you live together and everything."

"We don't live together, we share an Airbnb," I mutter, stepping back onto my treadmill. "And I'm not being weird about her. What about Paige? She's gotta have some pent-up aggression to take out on an axe."

"Nah, not her vibe."

"Serena?"

"Dance class."

"Reid and Abby must want a night out."

"No babysitter for Layla. Come on dude, just come! It'll be all four of us, so not like a date or anything."

I let out a sigh. I'm being ridiculous. "Fine. What time?"

Ethan gives me the details for tonight, and finally we get on with our workout. Thankfully he doesn't bring up Ashley or axe throwing again.

"I'm gonna fucking kill him," I mutter under my breath when the text comes in.

"Let me guess, Ethan just canceled?" Ashley comments drily. "Because I just got an apology from Summer, saying there's some issue at city hall and Ethan has to go into mayor mode."

I look up and nod. "Yeah. They aren't coming." I guess that must come out sounding a lot harsher than I intended, because her face falls slightly, making me wince.

"Is it really so bad if it's just the two of us?" she asks, so quietly I almost miss it. Damn, I really am being an asshole to her, and she doesn't deserve it. I'm ashamed of myself. This isn't how I treat women, hell, this isn't how I treat anyone.

"Nah, of course not. We'll have fun, no matter what," I say gamely. If I can somehow convince myself she's no different than any of my other female friends, this should be fine. The problem with that plan is, aside from two months in university with Mila, I've never once wanted to take any of my female friends and fuck them against a wall. And with Ashley, it's a toss-up from moment to moment if I want to take her to bed or put her on the first ferry back to the mainland.

But for now, I need to put that aside. My mom would kill me in my sleep if she knew I was ever anything less than a perfect gentleman to a woman. I didn't come by my charming reputation accidentally, after all. Ashley studies me for a second, then smiles, but it's brief and she's back to looking wary and uncomfortable. It's up to me, I guess, to show her I'm not going to be a total ass tonight.

"Come on, let's get signed in and start throwing shit."

I lead her over to the check-in counter, give the bearded guy wearing a plaid shirt our names, and pay for the two of us.

"You didn't have to pay for me," Ashley protests, but I just wave her off.

"I've got this. You just get ready to be humiliated by my axe throwing expertise."

That earns me a giggle. "Have you been here a lot?"

I turn to her with a wide grin. "Nope, never." There we go, easy. Charming.

She full on laughs, and we follow our hipster instructor over to our designated lane. Plywood lines the narrow space with metal fencing on top to keep everyone safe from rogue axes, I guess. At the end, there's a large bullseye painted on the wall. We both listen intently to the instructions we're given, and I'm all too aware of how close Ashley is, the smell of her perfume gently wafting up to me. All I would have to do is shift over slightly and I could brush against her, and I want to. But I won't.

Friends. Just friends. I can do this.

But when it's just the two of us, the awkward feeling is back. It's as if outside of work, we don't know how to act around each other. And I know it's my fault for being such a dick to her.

"Ladies first." I bow and step back, indicating Ashley should go. She stands on the line, and her body is stiff with tension and nerves. Her first throw falls way short of the back wall. Her second bounces off the wall.

"I suck at this," she states.

"Nah, you just need more power. Pretend it's my face on the bullseye."

An undignified snort comes out of her before she can stop it and she spins around, eyes dancing. Finally, there's the brightness I don't normally get to see, directed at me.

"Don't tempt me, Finn McNeil," she teases.

I just shrug and give her a smirk. "Go for it, princess. I don't mind."

She whirls back to face the target and lets her third axe fly. It hits the target, just outside of the bullseye. I start to clap, until she turns to fix me with a glare.

"Don't call me princess."

Okay...that seems like an over reaction to a nickname, but whatever.

Before we know it, our allotted time is up. And it's been fun, a lot of fun. Especially once we managed to get over whatever tension existed when we first realized we'd been stood up by the others. I impressed myself with my ability to put Ashley in the friend zone of my brain. Teasing her helped, and having her taunt me right back every time I missed the target only made me more determined to kick her ass. In the end, however, she proved to be an axe throwing pro, getting not one, but two near bullseyes, where I only managed one that hit semi-close to it.

When we're back in the car, heading down the highway to Dogwood Cove, it's a different vibe from the awkward drive up here earlier in the evening. Ashley is relaxed, much the way she was when I drove her home drunk from the bar, only this time I know she's only had one beer with me. Still, the silence between us is easy, and I don't even mind her ridiculous taste in music as much.

My eyes dart down at where her hand is resting on the center console. Out of nowhere I'm seized with the desire to pick it up, bring it to my lips and kiss it. Which is so unlike me, I actually shake my head in confusion.

"Everything okay?"

Shit, I didn't realize she saw that. Thinking quickly, I reply, "Yeah. Fine. Just thinking about something I need to do tomorrow."

She makes a soft sound of understanding, and silence falls again, and we stay that way for the rest of the drive.

I park in front of the Airbnb and Ashley immediately climbs out. I follow her up to the front door and into the dim hallway. She pauses outside her door. "I had fun tonight."

Who knows if she can see me smile, but I do. "So did I." I think I make out her nod, then she turns to open her door. Out of nowhere, my hand snaps out and wraps around her arm. "Wait."

My heart is pounding. I have no clue what's happening; it's as if my conscious mind is detached from my body, and I'm watching what I'm doing from the outside. She slowly turns to face me, my hand still wrapped around her delicate wrist. I swear I can feel her pulse fluttering under my fingers. But then again, maybe that's mine.

"Ashley, I…"

My words are cut off by the feel of her soft lips pressed against mine. Her free hand comes up to cup the back of my neck and with a groan, I drop her wrist and pull her into my body. I take the kiss deeper, feeling her mouth move with me. Her tongue darts out and tantalizes me, tormenting me with what I know

I can't have. I want to take my time, I want to explore her, find what makes her shiver and what makes her moan, but I can't. If all I get is this one kiss, I'm going to make it count. My hands move up to her shoulders and then to hold her face, angling it so I can nip her lower lip, that damn lip that has been teasing me for weeks. This kiss is unlike any other I've ever had in my life, and I've kissed plenty of women. There's a different sort of fire between us, something that has just been smoldering embers until now. But now it's burning hotter than a comet shooting across the sky.

A soft moan and the feel of her hand trailing down the front of my shirt jerks me back to reality. This is Ashley. I'm kissing *Ashley Elliott*, the one woman I've sworn to myself I can't have. I pull away, wrenching my lips from her skin.

"Shit."

I take a step back, my hand coming up to touch my lips, feeling the ghost of her lingering there. Her chest is heaving and her eyes are hooded. She looks needy and sexy, and entirely too fuckable. That kiss must have scrambled what few brain cells I have left because for the life of me I'm having a hard time thinking of one good reason not to kiss her again.

Pierre.

The winery.

Don't mix business with pleasure.

Okay, so some part of my brain must still be functioning. "We can't do this."

"Why not?" she asks, and the breathless tone of her voice has a thread of challenge to it that is so damn sexy.

"Because we work together."

"So? I'm not asking you to marry me, Finn." Now her hands are on her hips, and that challenge is morphing into something else. Anger, and rejection. Damnit.

"Ashley, we just can't. I'm sorry. I should have never touched you." I take another step back until there's enough space between us that I can feel my control slowly slipping back into place.

Ashley lets out a noise of frustration. "Yeah, you know what, you shouldn't have. Good night, Finn."

The slamming of her door shouldn't sting as much as it does.

Two hours later I'm lying in bed, wide awake, staring at the ceiling, contemplating just how badly I've fucked things up. One thing is for certain, if Ashley didn't think I was an asshole before tonight, she does now.

Well, I've already dug my own grave, might as well lie in it. If she hates me, it might make it easier to avoid her.

Letting out a muffled groan of frustration, I force myself to shut my eyes.

Tomorrow is gonna suck.

Chapter Twelve

Ashley

I could be mistaken, but it takes two consenting and actively participating adults for a kiss to be *that* explosive. And there's no doubt that Finn was eager with his *participation*. So why the *hell* did he have to pull such a fast one-eighty that my head was still spinning an hour later?

"We can't. We work together. Blah, blah, bullshit," I mutter under my breath as I get dressed the next morning. Clearly, I'm still not over the brush-off he gave me last night after what was undoubtedly the hottest kiss of my life. Knowing that I'm going to see him in less than an hour doesn't help. He disappeared early this morning; I guess he was able to sleep well enough to get up at his usual time of dead o'clock. I, on the other hand, tossed and turned all night long, debated pulling out my vibrator and finishing what he started, but decided not to take the risk of him hearing the noise. So basically, I'm grumpy, tired, and horny, and the last thing I want to do is go to work and see *him*. But today is the day the flooring gets installed, so I need to be there.

Plus, Pierre apparently had a question about the furniture that recently arrived.

When I arrive at the winery an hour later, I'm no less grumpy despite the coffee and scone I picked up from Mila on the way. Summer was there, and full of apologies for missing axe throwing. I guess I came across frustrated because both of them asked if anything was wrong, and when I barked at them, saying that I was just fine, Mila ignored my mood and insisted I come over tonight for a glass of wine. Not one to turn down drinks with friends, I agreed. Even though I know I'll probably have to explain a few things.

"Ashley, good morning!" Pierre's voice carries across the parking lot. I give him a wave in return as I unload my car. "Finn, can you help Ashley?"

My head jolts up, narrowly missing the hatch of my trunk. "No, no. I'm fine, Pierre. Really." I scramble to try and pick up everything I need to take inside.

"Let me help."

Finn's gruff voice sends shivers down my spine. Damnit. He's way too close to me; his warm, manly smell making my insides turn to goo. My only option is to say nothing and let him carry things inside. That should put some distance between us, I hope. In silence, I hand him the chair cushions I was unloading, and I grab the box of coasters I had designed as a surprise. Pierre showed me the logo they were thinking of, and I took a chance, making a few artistic changes before ordering a small batch of disposable coasters. If they don't like them, it's fine, but I'm hoping they'll see how it will go with the whole feel of the tasting room.

Inside, the construction crew is already hard at work and the space is filled with the sound of hardwood floor being installed. I take a minute and survey the room. The warm rust colour on the walls has already transformed it from a blank industrial building to a cozy, intimate space. The light floors tone well with the walls and brighten the entire place. Once the lighting is complete, furnishings and décor is set up, the room will be the perfect blend of elegant and eclectic. Truly, it's my dream space. Nothing I've worked on to date has so closely embodied my aesthetic.

"I wasn't certain the flooring would work with the paint, but Ashley, you have done it. It is, parfait." Pierre makes a cliché chef's kiss of admiration with his hand as he walks over. "Truly, when your father asked if I could use your talents, I knew that you would be the right person for our winery. My instinct. It is never wrong." He taps the side of his head with an enigmatic smile.

"I appreciate the opportunity to work on this project, more than I can ever say," I answer honestly. I may have come to this job because of Pierre's friendship with my father, but it really is Pierre I have to thank. He took a chance on me, not knowing my design style or skill level, and I'll never forget that. Even if it is mildly embarrassing my business opportunities had dipped so low, I needed dear old dad to step in.

"And are you enjoying your time in Dogwood Cove? It is a lovely town."

"Yes." I smile. "It's a beautiful place."

"Pierre, the truck is here with the latest batch of Chardonnay juice. I'll be in the barn for the day."

I force myself not to react to Finn's voice.

"Ah, wonderful. Have you shown Ashley the process for creating your magic yet?"

Oh Lord, no. Please no. Don't do this to me...

"Not yet."

Geez, does Finn have to sound so reluctant. My head lifts up of its own accord and I frown at him.

"Perhaps this is the perfect opportunity. Ashley, you really should learn how Finn crafts our exquisite wine from nothing but juice."

"It's not *nothing* but juice," Finn comments, and I hate the warmth and amusement he shows Pierre that he apparently can't show me. "But yes, Ashley, if you want to come and see how it's done, you're welcome to do so."

Seriously, am I the only one who can hear how unenthusiastic he is about the idea?

"Fine. Thanks." Pierre frowns at my clipped response, but I ignore him, picking up my coat and shrugging it on before I follow Finn out into the cold. The walk to the red barn that houses the fermenting tanks and whatever else Finn needs for his *magic* is thankfully short.

Inside are huge steel tanks, and the sweet smell of fermentation fills the air. Everything is gleaming, clean, and organized. I can see a long hose attached to one of the tanks and a man is busy with some controls I can't make sense of. Finn gives him a nod of greeting as he leads me briskly down the middle of the row of tanks.

"This is where the juice ferments. I add yeast to adjust sweetness and encourage the natural process. Eventually it'll go into barrels to be aged until it's ready to be bottled. Most of this will go to straight oaked chardonnay, but I'll pull some to put into our proprietary blend."

I have to speed walk to keep up, which I know he's doing on purpose. Still, it's interesting walking around and seeing the inner workings of a winery for the first time.

"I've never really liked the oaky flavour of chardonnay." Apparently, that's the wrong thing to say, judging by the scowl Finn gives me.

"It's an acquired taste."

I come to a stop. When he turns around, my hands are on my hips, and you better believe I'm glaring right back.

"Look, I get it. You don't want to be doing this right now. But do you really have to be such an asshole?"

He has the decency to seem chagrined, but that doesn't stop my rant now that I'm started.

"We kissed. It was great, at least for me it was. But if you want to pretend it didn't happen, fine. I'm here to do a job, not start dating or fall in love. So we'll chalk last night up to a mistake, or whatever. It was just a kiss. The least you could do is act like a decent human being."

"It was more than great."

My eyes widen. "Excuse me?" Out of everything I just said, *that's* the part he holds on to?

He looks up at me, and the scowl that had me feeling so mad at him has been replaced by a smoulder that should be illegal. "You heard me."

I swear the temperature in the room just went up ten degrees. My cheeks are warm, and my heart is pounding so loudly, I'd be shocked if Finn can't hear it. But before I can formulate any type of a response, the moment is broken by someone else yelling down the length of the barn.

"Hey Finn, we're all done unloading the tanks."

Finn turns to face the man who's come up to us, oblivious to the fact that I was seconds away from doing something embarrassing, like grabbing Finn and kissing him. Good grief, I can only imagine how well that would be received by the man who can't seem to decide if he wants to snap at me or flirt with me.

"Okay, I'm coming." He turns his head over his shoulder at me but doesn't make eye contact. "There you go. That's how we make wine." Then he's gone, and I'm left slightly less clueless about how white wine is made, but a lot more clueless about Finn McNeil.

By the time I get to Mila's house, I'm completely fried from overthinking every second Finn and I spent together. What the hell did he mean by "more than great?" Why would he even say that if he didn't want to do it again?

Gah! I'm so freaking confused.

"You look like you need a drink." I glance up from where I'm putting my keys into my purse to see Abby walk up beside me on the sidewalk outside Mila's house.

"I certainly do," I reply.

"Same. I never realized running a farm involved so much damn paperwork. Pretty sure I'm going cross-eyed."

"A...farm? Did you say a farm?"

Abby laughs. "Oh yeah, I forget you aren't from around here." At the look of confusion I'm sure I'm giving her, Abby reaches out a hand to touch my arm. "Take that as a compliment, you fit in so well with everyone. Anyway, I moved back here to help my Uncle Steve. He has a farm just outside of town. We grow pumpkins, Christmas trees, and some fruit. And we've got some animals, so we host school tours and stuff as well. I honestly had no clue what I was in for when I came over to help him out. But damn, licenses and permits and food orders and vet bills. It just never stops."

I have no clue what to say, so I just make a random noise that I hope conveys sympathy. Thankfully, Mila opens her door just as we step up to it. "Get in here, ladies, there's wine in the kitchen and gossip to share."

Mila's vibrant energy reminds me so much of Sarah. She left Vancouver right before I found my ex Tyson cheating on me, in fact. She almost flew back from Toronto to beat his ass up, but I told her not to be stupid. He wasn't worth it, and he never was. She moved for her dream job, and even though I miss her, I know she needed to leave. Hanging out with these ladies is a pretty good alternative, though.

Over a couple of glasses of wine and some amazing puff pastry things Mila made, I gradually feel the stress of the day lift away. It's been so long since I had a group of friends to relax with, I forgot how much fun it is when women get together and just laugh. Paige, with her serious nature and pragmatic approach to things, shouldn't fit with the chaotic conversation flowing around us, but she does and the one-liners she contributes are pure gold. Serena has dragged Summer up from her seat and is trying to teach her how to twerk, much to all of our amusement.

When the song finishes, Serena and Summer drop back down to the couch. "Alright, alright. You can't avoid it anymore, Ashley." Summer's eyes are dancing. She obviously doesn't realize quite how reluctant I am to talk about Finn. "We know something's going on. So spill."

"To be fair, we don't know anything for certain," Paige interjects, pushing her tortoiseshell glasses up on her face. "However, we have all observed clear signs of a significant attraction between you and Finn."

"And you guys were all alone at axe throwing. Tell me something happened," Mila adds.

Serena clasps her hands over her chest. "He's so damn sexy, and *hello*, free wine. You better get in on that."

"What's that face for?"

Crap. Guess I'm not as good at hiding my reactions as I thought. "Nothing. I just don't get what the big deal is. Yeah, he's attractive, but he's also a total ass."

Mila gives me a strange look. "Umm, hello, are we talking about the same person? Finn McNeil couldn't hurt a fly, loyal, generous to a fault, complete charmer — that Finn?"

I shrug, uncomfortable with how she's describing him. "That's not been my experience at all. He's been pretty rude and scowly to me, and gives more mixed messages than a magic eight ball."

Now they're all staring at me like I'm crazy.

"Wow. Ashley. That's weird. Like, really weird," Summer says. "Finn's a great guy. Tons of fun, total charmer and ladies' man. I've never heard him described as scowly."

I fold my arms over my chest. "Well, I guess I'm just lucky then."

"He has romantic feelings for you."

My traitorous heart skips a beat at Paige's simple statement. "Haha. I don't think so."

"No, I think Paige might be on to something," Mila says slowly. "I'm not sure why he would act rude and scowly as you put it; that's definitely not the Finn we're used to. I do know he was in some kind of relationship in California, and Ethan's mentioned it didn't end well, but I haven't seen him with anyone since he moved back. He and Reid used to go to Victoria to meet women." She winces apologetically at Abby, who's dating Reid. "Sorry, girlfriend but it's true. They aren't players, but when they wanted a hookup, they went outside of town so it wouldn't be awkward. Anyway, that means I honestly don't know how Finn would behave around a woman he's interested in. All I can say is, the way he looks at you, that man wants in your pants."

I chew on the inside of my cheek, thinking about what she's saying. I have no clue what gives them that idea, that Finn wants to be with me, but they do know him better than I do. Still...it doesn't add up. "I don't know what you guys see, but honestly he treats me like nothing more than a co-worker. And I'm only here for a few weeks." I almost admit that we kissed, but choose not to. There can't be anything good that comes from fueling their idea that Finn and I should be together.

Thankfully, I'm saved from having to say anything more by Abby. She shoots me a sympathetic glance before standing up. "Who needs more wine before we talk about the book?"

But for the rest of the evening, and even when I get back to the Airbnb courtesy of a ride from Ethan and Summer, I'm consumed by what Paige and Mila implied. And I'm confused by the hot and cold vibes Finn keeps throwing off. Part of me is sorely tempted to just barge into his room and confront him. But the fear of rejection, especially given my recent track record with relationships, is just too great.

Besides, in a few weeks, my job will be complete, and I'll have to head back to the city and try to figure out what I'm doing with myself.

Or you could stay.... It's not the first time the idea has occurred to me, especially since Tom mentioned looking for a partner. But my father, my life — at least what's left of it, is in Vancouver.

Not here.

CHAPTER THIRTEEN

Finn

The weird thing about the West Coast is that one day it can be cold and raining, and the next it can be weirdly mild and sunny. Today is one of those rare sunny days, and since most of the snow and slush is gone, Ethan and I decided to take advantage of us both having an afternoon off to hit the trails for a hike.

"You and Summer need a dog," I tease when we stop for a water break. "Maybe then you'd get more exercise and could keep up better." Ethan just rolls his eyes. He knows the truth is he's in better shape than any of us guys.

"You sound like my sister. Ever since she found her mutt, she's been on me about opening an animal shelter in town."

"Well, you are the big important mayor; it's up to you to take care of the citizens of the town, both human and otherwise."

"Fuck off, you idiot."

We both chuckle and I take another drink of water. Days like this are why I was so excited to move to Dogwood Cove. California was beautiful, but recent wildfires had put so many vineyards out of business and ruined much of the landscape. And the friends I had down there were different. There was no easy teasing and laughing like there is with Ethan and the guys. Down there, status is everything. It was too much.

We grab our packs and head back out on the trail to the lookout that gives an amazing view of the coastline of Vancouver Island and the Strait of Georgia. An hour later, we drop down onto a rock and stare out at the endless stretch of water. In the distance, you can just make out the edge of the mainland with all of the smaller islands dotted in between. It really is a spectacular sight.

"Care to tell me why my fiancée came home the other night and started bugging me about you supposedly being an asshole to Ashley?" He says it so casually it takes me a minute to register the words.

"I'm not...I don't..." There's no sense in hiding from Ethan. He knows me better than anyone. "Shit."

"Is this still about that girl down in Napa?"

"Look man, last time I got mixed up with someone connected to my work, I lost my fucking job. That can't happen this time. The winery is too important."

Ethan stands up and rolls his neck from side to side before fixing me with a critical glare. "Okay, fine. Don't get mixed up with her. But do you have to be an ass to her?"

"I don't mean to."

"Seriously, you sound like a fucking teenager. You don't mean to? Last time I checked you were an adult, fully in charge of your own actions. So man up already. Ashley's a great person, and she doesn't deserve you making her feel like crap because of your own issues."

Every word he says is true and makes me feel like a piece of shit.

"No woman deserves that, and I know you know that. Not to mention, acting like a tool isn't the best way to get her on your side. Especially not if you're into her."

My eyes shoot up to meet Ethan's. "I'm not into her," I blurt out quickly, too quickly, given Ethan's reaction.

A grin stretches across his face. "Yeah, you are. And everyone can see it except you, apparently. She's not the waitress, Finn. Dating her isn't going to cost you the winery."

"She's leaving soon."

"So?"

"So...I dunno. What if she doesn't want something casual?"

"What if she does? Or what if she stays? Or what if you stop being a pathetic excuse of a man and start treating her with respect and see what happens."

I know he's right. She deserves respect and so much more. And I am into her. Way more than I should be, way more than I expected to be. Ashley Elliott is under my skin and fills my head with dirty ideas. Keeping her at a distance seemed like the best possible way to avoid acting on those ideas, especially once I had a taste of her.

But I feel terrible that I've apparently been so good at pushing her away, I've come across as an asshole. Clearly my plan to think of her like any of my other female friends failed in the face of how attracted to her I am.

New plan. Man up, as Ethan said. Treat her with respect, and nothing more.

The Grab-n-Go is one of those small-town grocery stores that could never exist anywhere else. Stepping into it feels like a bit of a time warp, with its fluorescent lighting and layout that hasn't been updated in decades. But it's got everything I need, and there's bigger stores a short distance away in Westport. One thing that is really bugging me about my house still not being fixed is the lack of kitchen space. Sure, there is one at the Airbnb, but it's not the same as my own. And any time I cook there, I feel guilty for not offering food to Ashley. Granted, she's rarely home at the same time as me, and when she is, she's kept her bedroom door closed, so it's not like I have ignored her anytime I've made dinner.

Tonight I'm just getting a few essentials that I can turn into quick meals. The reality is, I eat breakfast at the bakery most days, and lunch tends to be whatever I have on hand at the winery. Protein bars, shakes, easy stuff that I can get down quickly in the middle of my workday. But I miss making a full dinner. Even cooking for just myself, there is something so satisfying about taking a pile of ingredients and creating a meal.

Tossing a package of beef jerky into my basket, I scan the shelves, searching for something to satisfy my sweet tooth. My weakness for candy isn't something many people know about and I pride myself on eating healthy most of the time. But there's something about Twizzlers, or jelly beans, that is just so damn satisfying in the evening. Grabbing a bag of each, I walk to the end of the aisle and turn into the next one, only for my footsteps to come to an abrupt halt. At the other end of the aisle, Ashley is reaching up to get something off the top shelf, and her sweater is riding up, revealing a sliver of skin that shouldn't be as tantalizing as it is. I take a step forward to help her, but she pulls down whatever she was after and turns away before I can get to her.

That's fine. I'm not really wanting to see her right now, anyway. Honestly, I'm still so damn confused by my conversation with Ethan earlier. Okay, I'm attracted to Ashley. A lot. It's not just her beauty, it's her personality. Her warm kindness, her sense of humour, and the fire I see in her. And yes, rationally, I know Ashley isn't the same as Cassandra, the server from the winery that made me lose my job last year. Cass loved drama and couldn't accept the fact that I wasn't looking for anything serious. When she couldn't convince me otherwise, she decided to do what she did best and cause trouble. Ashley is way more down to earth and calm; I can tell. And hey, maybe the fact that she isn't staying in town for long would mean she's open to something casual.

But there's still Pierre to think of. He cares about her, and he's got some pretty traditional ideas and morals. I can't imagine him approving of me having a fling with Ashley, even if it were something we both wanted.

I pay for my groceries and head out to the parking lot, still lost in thought. Just as I reach my car, I hear a familiar voice cursing. Casting a look around, I see Ashley bent over the open hood of her car, that sweater riding up again. Fuck. I can't walk away from her. It's dark and cold, and obviously her car won't start. There's no way I would leave any woman in this kind of situation. I might be useless when it comes to the construction stuff that Ethan does, but even I know how to jumpstart a vehicle.

"Hey, Ashley, you need some help?" I call out after putting my groceries in the front seat of my car. Her head flies up so fast she hits it on the hood of her car, and I sprint over. "Shit, are you okay?"

She's rubbing a spot and frowning, and I have to hold back from wanting to touch her and make sure she's alright.

"Yeah. I'm fine. But maybe don't sneak up on someone in a dark parking lot." Her crabby response makes my lip twitch. I might be insane, but I'm starting to like it when she pushes back at me. She doesn't take any shit, that's for sure. It makes me want to push her buttons, tease her. If being a jerk to her didn't help me keep my distance, maybe making her annoyed with me so she stays away will work.

"Sorry. I didn't realize I was so sneaky; I was just coming to offer my help."

Ashley barks out a laugh. "That's funny. From what I hear, you're not the handiest of guys."

"I'll have you know, I'm pretty good with my hands."

Her eyes widen. "You did *not* just say that!"

I shrug. "Yeah, I did. Anyway, do you want me to jump-start you?" I wink, letting her know I realize I'm being over the top with innuendo. "Your car, I mean."

She makes a small growl of frustration that's actually adorable, and that's not a word I use often. "Yeah, fine. Thanks."

I nod and turn to walk back to my car. Once my back is to her, I reach down to adjust myself. Flirting obnoxiously is one thing, but letting her see that even when she's being snarky she still turns me on is another.

A few minutes later my engine is running, the jumper cables connecting it to Ashley's car engine holding strong. When I glance over at her, she's rubbing her hands up and down her arms, still wearing only that damn sweater.

"Don't you have a coat?"

Man, if looks could kill, I'd be toast.

"No, *Dad*, I don't. I wasn't exactly expecting this to happen. I thought I'd be home and in bed with my book club read by now." Her voice is dripping with sarcasm.

Opening the door to my backseat, I grab the spare hoodie I have in there from the gym and toss it over. She catches it easily. "Thank you."

Silence falls between us for a minute. I lean against my car and stuff my hands in my pockets. "What would you have done if I wasn't here?"

She bites her lip, her eyes downcast. "Called Mila or Summer, I guess. Or gone inside to ask if someone could jump me." She looks up, and narrows her eyes. "I know how to jump a car, too, Finn."

"Never said you didn't, princess."

"Don't call me that." There's a weariness to her tone that makes me pause.

"Why not?" I ask softly.

She seems to ponder my question, her eyes searching me for something, though I'm not sure what.

"It has some bad memories attached to it."

I know that's not the full answer, but I'll take it for now. "Noted. No more princess."

"Thanks."

I push off of my car, and gesture to hers. "Try turning on your engine now."

She slides in and turns the key, and her car comes to life instantly. "Thank you." She steps back out and comes to the front where I'm detaching the cables. I close the hood of her car and the hood of mine and toss the cables into my backseat.

When I turn around, she's standing in front of me, twisting the cuff of my hoodie in her hands. It's so large on her it swallows her up, but it also stirs something in me, an unfamiliar emotion I don't want to pay too much attention.

"Here, let me give you your sweatshirt back."

"Keep it 'til we get home."

She nods and her tongue darts out to moisten her lips and my eyes zero in on it.

"Ashley..." I don't know what I want to say or do right now, but my hand drifts up toward her face.

But she steps back, and she won't meet my gaze. My hand drops.

"Right, well, thanks again, Finn. See you later." She's in her car before I can say anything, and the next thing I know, I'm staring at her taillights.

I don't drive straight home. Instead, I drive around town, giving her time to get home and settled before I arrive. She made herself perfectly clear tonight. Ashley isn't interested.

Point taken.

Chapter Fourteen

Ashley

When I drove away from Finn last night, I could have sworn he seemed disappointed. There is not one thing on earth that confuses me more than that man. The entire drive back to our Airbnb I stewed on the hot and cold, back and forth, completely messed up attention he keeps giving me. One minute he's flirting and moving to touch me, the next he's telling me he can't do this — whatever *this* is. For Christ's sake, it's not like I'm asking him to marry me, just maybe not leave me so damn sexually frustrated every time I'm around him. It's as if my libido is directly connected to him, and the second he's in my periphery, I go nutso. Like damp panties, heart pounding, salivating nutso. Of course, so far he's managed to douse that fire pretty damn quickly with his childish behavior. We're not in high school anymore, and this back and forth behavior is ridiculous.

The truth is, I'm fed up. As much as I've found myself seriously considering moving to Dogwood Cove, taking Tom up on his offer to partner, and making a new life over here...Finn and his mixed messages have me reconsidering. Not that I would actually base a life decision on a man, but still. The thought of seeing him all the time and having to fight my attraction to him isn't all that appealing.

But where does that leave me? I'll be done with the tasting room in a couple more weeks, and I've got nothing waiting for me on the mainland except my dad. Over here, there's the promise of a job, there's new friends, and there's a peaceful life I never thought I would enjoy as much as I have been.

And then there's Finn.

Damn that fine-ass man.

Today the three of us, Pierre, Finn, and myself, are meeting at another winery to take a look at a bottle display rack they have for sale. I would have simply purchased it myself, but Pierre wanted to accompany me and talk with the other winery owner, and he's apparently convinced Finn to come along. Pierre is on board with my sustainable practice, especially once I explained to him that I refinish used items to make them unique to the space. Finn, with his tight grip on his wallet, should be happy as well, but when I mentioned we were going to look at some used items, he grimaced. Seriously, there's no pleasing the man.

The drive to the other winery takes an hour, and I'm really glad I insisted on driving myself. The idea of being trapped in a car for this long with Finn, given how frustrated I am with him right now, is more than I could handle. What even was that last night? The way he said my name, with what sounded suspiciously like desire in his voice — he wasn't playing fair.

This location we're visiting is downsizing, which is why they're selling off some of the equipment. Apparently, the owner is getting older and can't run it anymore. Part of me wonders if Pierre is considering it for another investment and that's why he wants to meet with the owner, but then again his hands are pretty full with La Lune Rouge. Still, there's no denying the beauty of this place, with rolling hills and fields of vines, even in the grey late winter light. Patches of snow are still on the ground, dotting the landscape with white.

"Climate change is hitting this place pretty hard."

I startle at Finn's words, not realizing he had come up beside me.

"What do you mean?"

He leans against the fence casually. "Grapes are picky. Fickle about things like soil and ambient temperature. It affects when they ripen, and when you have to harvest." Finn gestures to the fields in front of us. "It can even affect the quality of the grapes and the varietals you can consistently produce."

"Is that why you don't grow very many grapes at La Lune Rouge?" I ask. I've been curious about that ever since I started learning about winemaking. Estate wines can be more marketable because they're exclusive to that winery. But from what little I understand, Finn and Pierre are purchasing their raw juice from vineyards in the Okanagan, located in the interior part of British Columbia. Its an area rich in wineries and vineyards, producing a lot of amazing wines.

"Partly, yes. We don't have a lot of land at La Lune Rouge, and in order to produce enough grapes of enough varieties to really have a full complement of wines, we'd need about five times the space we currently have. And the climate on Vancouver Island is tricky to work with. The vineyards we're purchasing from are well established and produce incredible grapes year after year." He shrugs. "It's the best option to get our wines out there quickly."

"But don't you want to someday have your own wine that you produce from start to finish?"

A solemn look comes over Finn's face. It's an expression I've never seen on him before, and I wait quietly until he's ready to answer.

"Yes. Someday, we will. With grapes that I brought from my grandfather's winery in France."

Who knows why this snippet of Finn's history surprises me, but it does. "I didn't take you for the sentimental type," I blurt out. Unfortunately, my words land wrong on Finn.

When he frowns and stands up from where he was leaning against the fence, I realize I've hit a nerve. "Yeah, well, family is important to me."

He goes to walk away, and I put my hand out to stop him. "Wait, Finn, I'm sorry. I didn't mean to imply —"

He shrugs off my touch. "I know. It's fine. Let's just go and see what we're here to purchase."

I watch his long strides grow the distance between us, and I can't help but feel like he was letting me in, and this time I was the one who pushed him away.

If I was in a bad mood earlier, I'm in a worse one now. Finn has done nothing but glare and growl monosyllabic answers to any question I've asked of him. Pierre left us alone to look over the equipment and décor for sale, and while my inner designer is cheering at the amazing quality of the items available, the rest of me is fuming mad.

I said one thing. *One thing* that he took the wrong way and now he's being even more of an asshole to me than before.

When Finn wanders off down a hall, allegedly to find a bathroom, I stay in the empty room alone, my temper rising. Finally, logic and reason abandons me, and I go to find him and give him a piece of my mind. I go up a flight of stairs, not even paying attention to the amazing old-world art on the walls. I try the first door I come to, but it's a closet. Then I hear a tap running. Bingo. Another door down the hallway opens, and I'm waiting.

"You need to *stop* being a grumpy ass caveman right *now*, and work with me." My hand is smacking his chest with every word, forcing him to take a step back into the bathroom. But I'm so frustrated, and so focused on giving him a piece of my mind, I just follow, not thinking about how weird it might seem to follow a guy into a bathroom. "I'm trying to do my *job* and you're just being a growly jerk, and I'm done with it!"

"Ashley, wait!"

I freeze at the urgent tone in his voice, my hand in the air, as the door clicks behind me.

"Ah, fuck."

"What?"

He heaves an exasperated sigh. "The door is broken. If you hadn't been so intent on berating me, I could have stopped you from getting stuck in here with me."

"Broken?" I say dumbly, turning around and jiggling the handle. "How the hell is it broken?"

"Well, gosh, Ashley, I don't know. If I did, do you think I'd still be standing here?" he says, sarcasm dripping from his words.

God. He's sexy, even when he's being an asshole, and I hate the fact that my body is responding to him being such a jerk. In an attempt to hide my reaction, I cross my arms in front of me and glare at him. "You're not exactly Mr. Fix-It. Let me try." I turn back and examine the door. Sure enough, the handle doesn't seem to engage to open. "How did you get out the first time?"

"I didn't let it latch fully shut."

Well, shit.

My head drops down to the door that has sealed me in a small room with the man I'm beyond frustrated with, and beyond attracted to. "Seriously? We're stuck in here? What is this, some cheesy, made-for-TV movie? Get lost, Hallmark, this is my life!" I'm spiraling and I know it.

"Relax, would you? I'll just text Pierre for help," Finn says, and I hear him pull out his phone.

"His battery is dead, remember? He mentioned that before he went off with Oliver," I mumble, still facing the door.

"Fuck. Okay, I'll just climb out the window."

That makes me turn around. "And what, rappel down the wall like spider man?"

Finn opens the large window and looks down. "It's not a big drop. I can make it."

I walk over and look out myself. He's right, it's maybe only six feet down, thanks to the way the building is set into the slope. Still, jumping out a window onto cold, icy ground isn't my idea of a smart plan.

"But the ground is all slushy and that patch of snow seems hard packed. We could try calling out for someone," I offer.

Finn shakes his head. "There's no one else here, it's just us. It's fine, Ashley. I'll jump down, then walk around and open the door for you."

I watch as he climbs up onto the windowsill, worry gnawing at me. "Wait, Finn, you don't have to do this." My hand goes to his back and I feel the muscles underneath his shirt.

"Don't worry." He gives me a grin and a wink, then turns back to the window. One second he's there, the next he's not. But when I hear him cry out in pain, my heart leaps into my throat.

"Finn! Oh my God!" He's lying on the ground, clutching his knee. "Are you hurt?"

"Finn? Ashley? Where are you?"

"Pierre! Around the back!" I scream, watching Finn, who still hasn't said anything, he just groans. I can see him breathing in and out deeply. Pierre and Oliver come around the building, and Pierre rushes to Finn's side, kneeling on the wet ground.

"We got stuck in the bathroom upstairs and he jumped out of the window," I call down. Oliver, the winery owner, looks up at me.

"Oh dear, that door. I am so sorry." He hurries off, hopefully to come and let me out as I watch Finn slowly come to stand, leaning heavily on Pierre.

Sure enough, the bathroom door opens and Oliver is standing there, fretting and twisting his hands together. "I am so sorry, Ashley, I should have warned you both about the door."

"It's fine," I say as I rush past him, anxious to get to Finn. By the time I make it to the front of the building, Finn is sitting on a bench, still clutching his knee. I drop down to the ground in front of him and my hands cover his, making his head jerk up in surprise.

"Ashley, I'm fine."

"No, you're not." His voice is laced with pain, and I'm filled with mixed emotion. Guilt that he got hurt because of me, relief that it's nothing more serious, and a desire to take care of him. "I'm taking you to get checked out."

I stand and face Pierre. "Can you help him get to my car?"

Pierre gives me an enigmatic smile that I can't be bothered to make sense of. "Yes. You'll take good care of our Finn, won't you?"

I give him a brisk nod and hurry over to my car, which is thankfully nearby. Clearing off my front seat, I slide it all the way back to give him as much legroom as I can. Still, he winces when he gets in, and his head falls back onto the headrest. Given the way he isn't fighting me on this, I can tell he's really hurting.

All because of me.

Chapter Fifteen

Finn

The throb in my knee is drowning out everything else. It's the same leg I injured playing soccer my senior year of high school. All I can think of is, I hope to God I haven't torn the ligaments again because healing from that injury was hell. And I wasn't trying to launch a new business.

"I just feel so awful. Can I stop to get you some coffee or maybe some ice? Wait, I have a blanket in the back seat if you want it."

Ashley hasn't stopped fretting since we left Oliver's winery. For the most part, I've ignored her. I'm sure she means well, but I'm focused on holding my knee steady since any sudden movement is making it hurt even worse.

"I'm fine, Ash," I grit out between my teeth. "Honestly, just take me back to the Airbnb. I'll get some crutches tomorrow and I'll be fine." Okay, I'm lying. I know I'm not fine, I know I need to get checked out, but seriously, she needs to stop hovering.

Thankfully, we pull up to the Westport Hospital a few minutes later. I let Ashley come around to help me out of the car because the truth is, I need it. Slowly, we hobble to the main entrance, where Ashley manages to find a wheelchair for me. When she goes to push me inside, I wave her off. "I can do this."

She stands by silently, twisting her hands together as I check in with the triage nurse. When I'm done, we head over to the waiting area and Ashley sits down in a chair beside me. "You don't have to wait, Ash," I say, stifling the curse of pain I want to let out.

"That's the second time you've called me Ash," she says it so quietly, I almost miss it over the noisy waiting room.

"Is that okay?"

She turns and smiles at me softly. "Yeah, I like it. And I'd like to stay, if you don't mind."

No, I don't mind. It's oddly comforting having her here with me. My knee still throbs, making me feel nauseous from the pain and worried I might have done some real damage. But Ashley wanting to stay, having someone care about me this way, it feels good.

"Thank you."

When I feel her cover my hand that's clutching the handle of the wheelchair with a death grip, I sense my entire body relax at her warm touch. Turning my palm up, I thread my fingers with hers.

"I hate hospitals," I state in a low voice. My words are punctuated by a low moan from someone else in the ER. Ashley's fingers squeeze mine lightly and I tip my head up to look at her, my eyes darting over her face as if I'm seeing it for the first time. And in a way, I feel like I am. I'm seeing more than just her beauty, I'm seeing her kindness and compassion. Even though I have been embarrassingly harsh toward her, she's here with me.

"I'm sorry I've been such an ass."

I see a flicker of surprise dance across her face.

"It's fine. You didn't want me here, I get it."

"No," I start to say, then I'm overtaken by a jolt of pain when I move my leg wrong. "Fucking hell. Sorry. Shit, I'm screwing this up." My hands move to cup my knee, massaging my quad which is tense from everything. I don't miss the fact that I wish she was touching me somehow, but that thought is overwhelmed by the agonizing throb in my knee.

"Finn, you don't need to apologize right now. It's fine, I'm fine. Let's just focus on you." Her hand flutters down onto my shoulder and rubs back and forth gently. "Tell me about California. No wait, tell me about France. You mentioned you used to go there to visit family?"

I know she's just trying to distract me, but hell, anything is better than focusing on the tense energy around us, the sick and injured people, including myself, or the weird antiseptic smell of the hospital.

"Yeah. For years we would go to France to spend time with my mom's family there. Sometimes we'd hop over to Scotland on the way to see Dad's family, but I much preferred France. My grandfather owned a vineyard there, and the freedom I had was like nothing else. Days of just being outside, running around and playing. My cousins and I would play hide and seek in the vines, and my grandfather would set up scavenger hunts for us all over the property. Little notes that I couldn't read very well because they were all in French." I chuckle at the memories. "I went home and begged my mom to teach me more than what I was learning in school, so I could keep up with my cousins. The next summer I went back and shocked them all."

"It sounds like you have a lot of good memories."

"Yeah." We fall silent, and in the quiet I realize something. The distraction worked. My leg still hurts like a son of a bitch, but I'm a lot more relaxed. But something tells me some of that is also thanks to Ashley and her warm, comforting presence. Of course, my body chooses this moment to crash from the adrenaline high of my fall, and in an instant I'm more exhausted than I have been in years. I slump back against the hard back of the chair, grateful that we've got space in our little corner of the waiting room for my injured leg to be stretched out.

"Tired?" Ashley asks softly, proving just how intuitive she is. I nod. My eyes are heavy, my limbs are heavy, and even though my knee is still killing me, I just want to sleep.

"Close your eyes. If the doctor comes, I'll wake you up." Ashley gives me a comforting smile. "You can even rest your head on my shoulder if you want. Acting as your pillow feels like the least I can do right now."

I don't let myself think about it, I just take her up on the offer and lower my head down to her shoulder, letting myself give in to the pain-induced fatigue. The only thought that I can't push away is the fact that Ashley is finding her way past all of the walls I had built to keep her at a distance, and I'm surprisingly okay with that.

The sensation of a warm hand stroking my cheek slowly brings me back awake.

"Finn, the doctor is ready for you."

"Mmm, Ash," I mumble as my head turns into her neck. She smells good. Wait, what? I jolt upright. "Shit." My leg. Goddamnit, my leg.

"Are you okay?" Ashley's hands comes to my back.

"Yeah," I grind out. "Let's get this over with."

Three hours later, we're finally on our way home. I'm wearing a pair of shorts the social worker at the hospital gave me when the doctor had to cut off my jeans, and thank God for small mercies. The idea of being in a hospital gown in front of Ashley makes me shudder.

My knee is fine, no major injury. The doctor thinks I just twinged the old injury. Rest and compression as needed, and hopefully I'll be fine soon. It could have been worse, but I'm still frustrated by the injury. Ashley and I haven't talked about how we held hands in the waiting room, she'll barely even make eye contact with me. And I'm feeling a bit lightheaded and tired from the painkillers they gave me, making me next to useless. But even in my doped up state, I'm aware of her. The change in energy between us is palpable, like a warm current connecting us instead of the electric static that pushed us apart.

As we cover the short distance from Ashley's car to the house, she hovers beside me as I crutch to the front door. The fact that she's so concerned for me could come across as annoying, but it doesn't. It just shows me how kind she is. Maybe it's my decreased inhibitions from the drugs, but I'm starting to wonder just how bad it would be to cross that line with her. Take the chance on mixing business with pleasure.

When we make it to my door, Ashley reaches in front of me to twist the handle and open it. Her hair brushes my chin and I stifle a groan. Whoever said drugs make it harder to get turned on is insane.

"Okay, let's get into bed." Her eyes flash up to me in horror and I hide my smirk. "You. Let's get *you* into bed. Wait, that's no better. Oh my God. Get into bed." She claps her hand to her forehead. "Shit. You know what I mean."

I decide to take pity on her. "Yeah, I do. It's fine, Ash." I hobble my way over to the bed, then sit down carefully. She rushes over and lifts my leg by the heel and I flash her a grateful smile.

"Thank you. For everything."

The look she gives me is full of such warmth and compassion, I almost miss the flicker of desire hiding in her eyes. But make no mistake, I see it. It's there. And that alone is what makes me bold enough to take her hand again, threading my fingers through hers like I did at the hospital. Her gaze drops down to our joined hands, then back up to my face.

"What are you doing, Finn?" she asks softly.

My thumb strokes back and forth across her knuckles before I answer truthfully, "I don't know."

Her tongue darts out to lick her lips and that's it. My restraint snaps. Any trace of fogginess from the painkillers is gone and I am all too aware of this moment in time. The hand that isn't entwined with hers comes up to cup the back of her head. Keeping my eyes on her so there's no mistaking my intent, I draw her closer.

"Ask me again."

Her pupils dilate. "What?"

"Ask me what I'm doing." The words come out as a growl. I'm barely holding back. She's so close.

"What...what are you doing Finn?" she breathes.

"Kissing you."

I cover her gasp with my mouth. Her lips part and I take the invitation, sliding my tongue inside. She pulls her hand free from mine and her fingers slide through my hair. Our tongues tangle together as I grasp her hips and pull her over to straddle my lap. When she feels my cock, rigid between my legs, she moans into our kiss, taking it deeper. Her hips start to move and I find myself needing to count backwards from one thousand to try and control myself.

"Ashley," I tear my lips away from hers, earning a whimper that does nothing for my self-control. "Babe."

"Mmm," she purrs and my grip tightens. Her eyes slowly blink open and she looks at me with unmistakable need in her eyes. "What?" she pants. Her hair is mussed from my hands, her lips are swollen from my kisses, and she's by far the most stunningly sexy woman I have ever seen.

"I just want to make sure you're okay with this."

Her gaze softens, but her lips turn up in a sassy smirk. "Finn. If I wasn't okay with kissing you, do you really think I'd be sitting where I am right now?" She gestures down to where our bodies are intimately touching.

I chuckle, and the vibration of the sound makes her eyes darken. Slowly, she lowers her head to meet mine.

"Kiss me."

Happily. This time when her hips start to grind down on me, I cautiously lift mine, making sure not to put too much weight on my bad leg. Fuck yes. My hands travel down the sides of her body and back up again. She's holding herself up with her palms on my chest and I want to rip my shirt off so I can feel her touch on my bare skin. But when she lifts one hand off, takes mine, and slides it up under her sweater so I can cup her breast, that need to feel is satisfied. My lips travel down her neck, and I suck gently at the base of the slender column.

"Finn," she moans, and the sound of my name, laced with her desire, is the hottest thing I've heard. I want to hear it again, only louder.

The obnoxious sound of my phone makes Ashley jerk back. "Ignore it," I mumble against her skin. Nothing is going to make me stop. I lift my head, and she intuitively obliges, tilting back so I can lift her shirt up and over her head. When my eyes fall on her lace-covered breasts, I say a silent thank you to whatever universal power conspired to create this moment in time. But just as my hands are about to unclip her bra, my fucking phone rings again.

"Fuck." My hands drop; the moment is lost. I fall down to the pillow.

"You should answer it." Ashley nervously picks up her shirt and puts it back on. "It might be important."

Nothing is more important than what we were doing, I think to myself, but she's right, it's weird for someone to call back-to-back like that. Caller ID tells me it's Ethan, which makes it even more strange. He rarely calls.

"Ethan? You okay?" I say in greeting, one hand resting on Ashley's leg.

"Am I okay? I'm fine, but what the hell happened to you? Ashley texted Summer that she wasn't going to be able to meet up with her because you were at the hospital. Dude!"

Ashley winces and mouths an apology which I dismiss with a gentle shake of my head. I squeeze her thigh so she knows I'm not upset about her saying anything. Ethan is still rambling and I check back in to the conversation.

"...something about falling out of a window. Seriously?"

"Yeah, I fell out of a window and hurt my knee, but I'm fine."

"*How the hell did that happen?*" Ethan yells and I hold the phone away from my ear. When he gets worked up and worried about someone, Ethan goes full-out.

Ashley lets out a small sigh and my hand comes up to cover my eyes. "I'm just, yeah. I'm gonna go," she whispers, as she climbs off of me, my dick weeping at the loss of contact. I should say something, but she's slipped out the door faster than I can come up with anything.

"Goddamnit, Ethan," I growl into the phone, my head falling back on the pillow.

"Wait. I heard a door close. Was that Ashley? Hold on, did I interrupt something?" His voice has gone from full of concern to dripping with amusement, the fucker.

"Thanks to you, not enough," I grumble in reply. Ethan's deep laugh irritates the shit out of me. At the same time, maybe his interruption is a good thing. Not that I'm regretting what happened, hell no. The lid is off Pandora's box now, and there's no containing what's inside. But Ashley deserves better than some quick fooling around while I'm high on painkillers.

"Oh man, I'm sorry, dude. I had no idea. But seriously, though, are you okay?" Ethan asks, and all trace of laughter is gone. "Is it your bad knee?" He knows all about the injury in high school, seeing as I complained about how it ruined my chance at a scholarship for soccer in university.

"Yeah, it is. But it's fine. Well, it will be." I wince as I shift in bed, completely contradicting my words. "Nothing some rest and ice won't help."

"Let us know if we can do anything." Ethan pauses for a beat. "Although, now that you've got a live-in nurse at your beck and call, maybe you won't need us."

"Fuck off," I shoot back at him. "She's not a nurse and she's not at my beck and call."

"Just your cock and call?"

"Who the hell are you and what did you do with my best friend?" I'm getting irritated now. Ethan isn't normally the one to tease this relentlessly, but then again, he's different since he fell in love with Summer. More relaxed and easygoing. Still, having the full blast of his teasing is getting to me. I'm tired and in pain, and I just want to get off the phone and find Ashley to figure out what the hell is going on between us.

"Sorry, sorry. I'll stop. I'm just glad you clearly aren't being an asshole to her anymore. Although hooking up with her isn't exactly what I had in mind when I told you to stop."

A groan escapes me. "Trust me, this isn't what I had in mind, either. It's not like I've got time for a relationship right now with the winery just getting up and running." I fall silent, thinking about that statement. "But it's also all I can think about. She is, I mean. It's fucked up, man, I know it. But Ashley's amazing. Even when she's angry at me, spitting fire at something I've said or done, she's amazing."

"Wow, dude."

"Yeah. I'm screwed," I say drily.

"Nah, you're falling for her. It's about time a woman made you see things differently. So what are you going to do about it?"

"That's the problem. I have no idea."

Chapter Sixteen

Ashley

The irony that I'm now doing exactly what I was mad at Finn for doing is not lost on me. Yep, I'm avoiding that man like the plague. It's been shockingly easy, seeing as Ethan showed up at the Airbnb yesterday with bags of groceries and who knows what else. Aside from a knowing smile, he didn't say a word, thank God.

Naturally, Finn didn't come to the winery yesterday or today, so I'm going on forty-eight hours of successfully dodging any interaction with him.

Is it immature and ridiculous? Yes.

Do I want to see him and finish what we started? Also yes.

Am I absolutely bone-deep terrified of what we started…abso-fucking-lutely, yes.

On my way home from Victoria where I was picking up a few finishing touches for the tasting room, I swing into Camille's, the café that is attached to The Nutty Muffin. Mila just opened the café a few months ago, but it's busy every time I go in, and today is no exception. Even now, in the early evening, almost all of the tables are full of people with sandwiches or bowls of soup. There's a guy playing guitar softly in one corner, and I have to admit — he's pretty good.

I place my order for a grilled chicken and veggie panini, and find an empty stool at the long counter to sit and wait. Its been a long day, and I'm tired. A quick and easy dinner and home to my bed is all I can handle thinking about right now.

"Hello, Ashley, how is Finn recovering from his injury?"

I swivel on my seat to face Paige. "Hi! He's, umm, well, he's okay, I think."

She pushes her glasses up her nose and frowns slightly. "You think? I assumed since you were now intimate with each other, you would know such a thing as how he is doing."

I choke on my sip of water. "Intimate?"

Paige gives me a quizzical look. "That's what Summer told Mila and I yesterday. Ethan allegedly interrupted a private moment between the two of you. Am I mistaken? Has the forced proximity of your living situation not created the perfect environment for romance?"

Good grief. Paige's blunt assessment might be a little too influenced by all of the steamy books she reads, but she's not wrong.

"I...don't know how to answer that," I admit.

"With the truth would be preferable."

"The truth is, yes, we kissed, but it didn't go any further, and I don't know if I want it to go further, or if he does. So I'm avoiding him and I don't know how he is right now." My chest is heaving after that word vomit. To her credit, Paige doesn't seem ruffled at all, she's still calmly looking at me as if I didn't just spill my guts to her.

"Ah, men. They just live to confuse the heck out of us. Let the record show, none of us are the least bit surprised to hear you and Finn kissed, my friend. The sparks between you two are pure fire."

Crap, I didn't even notice Mila walk over. She drops her arm over my shoulders. "Despite your 'he's so grumpy' complaints at book club, we all knew you guys would hook up eventually. So the question is, what the heck are you doing here and not at home playing nurse to your man?"

"What's the point? My life isn't here, it's in the city. And Finn has made it quite clear how he feels about dating someone he works with. What happened the other day was just because of heightened emotions from his injury. Nothing more," I blurt out. It might be oversharing, but damn it feels good to get things off my chest.

"Wait. You're not staying in Dogwood Cove?" The hurt I hear in Mila's voice makes me wince, but is also weirdly touching.

"I mean, I don't know. My dad is in the city, and I guess I just figured I would go back there when the tasting room is done." My voice trails off because the reality is, my life is *not* in the city anymore. I don't have an apartment, I don't have any clients, I don't even have any close friends, with Sarah living on the East Coast now. There's only my dad tying me to the mainland.

"But if you and Finn were really together, would you consider staying?"

I tug my lower lip between my teeth and think about what she said. Not that a man would ever be the sole reason for a major life change like moving, but there's more than just that. There's Tom and his offer of work, there's the peace and lower level of stress I feel being on Vancouver Island, and there's this — friends who care about me and want me to be happy.

"Who knows," I answer slowly. "I mean, I won't stay just for him, but I do love it here." The words sound wistful, even to my ears, and the answering smile on Paige's and Mila's faces solidify my wishful thinking into a more tangible desire. "I could be happy moving here."

Mila claps her hands together. "That's awesome. I really hope you do. And I can help you with somewhere to live. The apartment over the bakery is vacant, or Ethan and I have some rental properties. Ooh, or maybe you and Finn will fall madly in love and buy something, and then you'll both never leave!" Her voice has increased in pitch and volume, and I tug at her sleeve to try and get her attention, but it's futile.

"Mila, stop, you're making some very grand assumptions," Paige says chidingly.

I shoot Paige a grateful smile. "Yeah, I appreciate the enthusiasm, but one step at a time, okay?" Thankfully, Mila seems to get it, although she lets out a slightly disgruntled huff.

"Fine. But a year from now when you're living together, I'm going to say I told you so."

Emboldened by my conversation with the girls, and fueled by my panini and a toffee nut cookie from Mila, I drive back to the Airbnb. It's time to stop avoiding Finn and face what's happening between us head on. I can't exactly deny the fact that I'm attracted to him, even when he's being a growly, scowly jerk.

When I get home, the darkness that comes with short winter days is falling. I head inside and drop my coat and purse in my bedroom before going down the hall to Finn's room. The door is slightly ajar, and I knock lightly. There's no answer, but it's not like he could go anywhere right now, so I push the door open. What I find inside softens my heart toward him even more.

I tiptoe into the room and just look at him. He's sprawled on his back, one arm resting on his stomach and the other up by his head. His grey T-shirt has ridden up slightly, showing some tanned skin that rises and falls slowly with his breath. I can see his tattoos that snake down his arms, just begging for my fingers to trace them. His eyes are closed, those long lashes dusting his scruff covered cheeks. I carefully lift a blanket to cover him, and my hand drifts up to a lock of dark hair that has fallen over his forehead. Brushing it lightly aside, I feel a pang in my heart. I could easily fall for this man. Heck, I think I already am, despite everything.

"Ash?" His voice is rough with sleep. He blinks his eyes open, and there's such a sense of peace in his expression, I can't help but stroke my hand down his cheek.

"Hey. How are you feeling?"

His hand drifts up to hold mine against his cheek. "Better now that you're back." Well, damn. If that isn't what every woman wants to hear, I don't know what is.

"Is your leg sore?" I carefully sit down on the edge of his bed.

"Nah. Only when I move." His eyes are dancing, and with startling clarity, I realize that somehow he owns a piece of my heart already.

"Then don't move," I tease right back, squeezing his hand gently. He chuckles quietly and brings his other hand up to play with my hair that has fallen over my shoulder.

"Stay here tonight?"

The hesitant way he asks tugs at every corner of my heart. He's soft, open, vulnerable, and he wants me. I nod and slip off the bed. His hand grabs mine again and he looks at me questioningly.

"I'm just going to change," I say quietly. His head relaxes back on the pillow with a small smile.

I hurry to the bathroom to brush my hair, tie it back in a loose braid, and brush my teeth, then head to my bedroom to change into some pajama shorts and a tank top. In the middle of pulling my tank top over my head, I hear Finn slowly make his way to the bathroom. Crap. What do I do? Do I go to his room now? Wait 'til he's done? Time to overthink this as I do everything else. Just as I decide to go and wait for him in his room, I open my door to see him standing on his crutches in the hallway.

"I was just coming," I start to say, then stop when I realize the double meaning of the words I just said.

Finn raises his eyebrows in a sexy smirk. "I'll take care of that someday, Ash."

I blush furiously. "Oh God, I didn't mean it like that."

He chuckles softly. "That's fine, I did. But not right now. Can we just..." he trails off and stares down at the floor before taking a deep breath and looking back at me. "I don't want to push you or push us too fast. I just really want to hold you tonight."

Oh, my heart.

"Okay."

Together we slowly make our way into his room. I let Finn settle in bed first, but when he lifts the blankets beside him, I slide in. His arm reaches out and tugs me flush against his body so that my head is resting on his shoulder and my hand finds a place on his chest. I can feel the steady beat of his heart underneath me and when he kisses the top of my head, my lips curve into a smile.

"Is this okay?" he asks, and I nod. "Good. I just, I've noticed you're not the kind of girl who like, hugs everyone." I cringe. It's always a guess as to how someone will take the fact that I'm not big on physical affection with people who are just my friends or less.

"Yeah, it's weird, I know. I've just never really been affectionate with people other than my dad."

"Nah, not weird. I guess I just want to make sure that doesn't extend to cuddling with me."

I lift my head up to look at him, and think about it for a minute. He's serious about his concern, I can tell. "No, this is nice. I...I don't mind cuddling with you."

"Good. I don't mind cuddling with you, either."

I lay my head back down on his shoulder and feel him take a long breath in and out. I could overanalyze why I'm pretty sure I would love to hug Finn, but now's not the time.

"Thank you for being here," he whispers against my head before kissing me once more. I open my mouth to tell him it's not exactly a hardship, but when I look up, his eyes are closed. Faster than I thought it would, his breathing evens out into the peaceful pattern of sleep. When I glance over at his bedside table, I discover the culprit. He must have taken one of his painkillers, and that's why he's so drowsy and adorable. I snuggle in closer, and when his arm tightens around me, I let my own stress and worry fade away.

When my brain slowly makes its way to consciousness the next morning, I register two things immediately.

One, the warm, solid wall of muscle underneath me and two, the indescribable sense of happiness I feel. The first makes sense given my sleeping situation. The second baffles me. Since when does waking up with a man lead to such a complete feeling of everything being right in the world?

"Mmm." The sound of that contented sigh coming from Finn brings a goofy smile to my face. And when I feel his lips press against the top of my head, I lift my face to meet his. We kiss, both of us still in that dreamlike state that only an early morning and the magic of newfound intimacy can bring.

"You're here," he says, and his eyes are smiling at me.

"You asked me to stay."

"I know. I'm just really happy you did."

I don't know how to handle this softer, affectionate Finn. It's so at odds with the man I've experienced so far, the man who's either abrupt and rude, or flirtatious and full of life. My hand caresses his cheek, and he turns to kiss my palm. Feeling brave, I shift upward so I can kiss him. His hands come up to hold me against him. When his tongue licks the seam of my mouth, I open eagerly. It's so easy to get lost in his kisses and let the intoxicating connection between us take over. But then Finn moves to roll me over onto my back and before I can stop him, he cries out with a curse.

"Ow. Shit," Finn yelps, dropping back onto the bed. "Damnit, I'm sorry." He groans, closing his eyes in frustration. I run my hands through his hair and wait until he opens them again. Little does he know, he has nothing to apologize for. His injury just means we have to be careful, and maybe a little creative. A side of me I haven't set free in a long time, thanks to a lackluster sex life with my ex, is back and ready to go. My inner sensuality rises to the surface, and I give him my most flirtatious wink.

"It's okay, it just means I get to be in charge." Carefully, so I don't hit his knee, I straddle his waist. The expanse of muscle underneath me almost makes me salivate. I lift my shirt up and over my head, taking in the possessive look he gives me with an inner smile.

"Ash. You're stunning."

I lean over, letting my hair cascade around us, and kiss him deeply. His hands are still glued to my hips, so I press my breasts against his chest and slowly start to rock my pelvis against his. I trail my fingers up and underneath his shirt, teasing the skin I find there. Sitting up, I tug at the hem.

"This has to go."

We maneuver his shirt off and I take a minute to really appreciate the muscles that I saw only briefly during that ill-fated shower scene.

Oh, yes, please.

Chapter Seventeen

Finn

The way Ashley is staring at me is making me completely forget about my injury. That is, until I go to move. Fucking hell, this is torture. I'm all for a woman on top, but there are things I want to do to her, things that are infinitely more difficult now. But not impossible. As tempting as it is to go straight for the goods, I still want to take my time. Squeezing her hips gently, I use the abs that I spend way too long on developing at the gym to sit up and kiss her neck. When her head falls back with a little moan, I let my hands drift upward, noticing where she shivers at my touch. Slowly, painfully slow, I move my lips and hands around to her front until they meet at her gorgeous breasts. One hand cups and squeezes gently, while the other tips her chin down so I can kiss her, and make sure we're on the same page.

"If you're going to need me to stop, sweet girl, tell me now. Because once I get a taste of you, it'll be a hell of a lot harder."

The fire in her eyes sears me. "Don't stop, Finn."

Giving her a wolfish grin, I reach down to take her legs and encourage her to wrap them around me, bringing her snug against my body. Our bare torsos press together, and she starts to rub herself against my rock-hard cock trapped inside my boxers. I can't lift my hips much without putting pressure on my damn knee, but that doesn't seem to stop my fiery girl. She grins down on me, taking my lower lip between her teeth and tugging gently. I wrap my hands in her long hair and tug her head back until she releases my mouth with a pop. "Easy there, babe. You might be on top, but that doesn't mean I'm giving up all control."

I bend slightly and take one breast in my mouth, biting down gently on her hard nipple before soothing it away with a kiss. Judging by her moans, and the way her hands are gripping my shoulders, she's enjoying that, so I move to the other side and give it the same treatment.

"Oh my God, yes," she breathes as I lightly suck and nip and kiss my way around her chest. But I need more.

"Take off your shorts," I say, unable to hide the rumble of arousal lacing my words. Ashley's eyes widen, but she lifts her hips and shimmies off her shorts. "Fuck. Ash." The sight of her sex, glistening with all the evidence of her desire, is making my dick literally ache. But I need to taste her. I lay back down and place my hands on her perfect ass, pulling her toward me. It takes a second for her to understand what I'm asking, and when she does, she looks down at me with no small amount of uncertainty.

"Finn. I'll smother you."

"What a hell of a way to die." I smirk, earning an eye roll and a giggle. I smack her ass lightly. "Get up here and give me what I'm waiting for, woman."

"Oh, good grief. You're demanding in bed," she teases, but she makes her way up the bed until she's almost exactly where I want her. I give her one more wicked grin.

"Demanding, yes. But I think you'll find I'm also very, very generous."

Then with a firm grip on her hips, I pull her up the last bit so that she's straddling my face. Her hands come to the headboard and she peers down at me with a worried, yet sensually curious expression on her face.

"I've never done this before."

"Me neither," I answer honestly. "But I can't fucking wait." I punctuate my statement with the first swipe of my tongue up her slit, and goddamn, she tastes like heaven. Her sweet, wet heat engulfs me, and it's by far the hottest thing I've ever experienced. Her initial gasp of surprise gives way to soft moans, and her hips start to undulate over me. My tongue slides over her folds, exploring her, tasting her. With her thighs clamped tightly around my head, the soft flesh of her ass under my hands, and her dripping wet core right over my face, I'm surrounded by Ashley. It's a multisensory experience. All I can do is taste her, smell her, hear her, and feel her.

I start to slowly thrust my tongue in and out, mimicking the movement I plan on doing with my cock next. I change it up, sucking her lips into my mouth, feeling them swell.

"Oh God," she cries out, leaning back so her hands find my stomach, her fingers curl into my abs, and her hips start to thrust into my face. It's dirty, but perfect. I want this to last forever, I want to stretch out this moment of pleasure to last a lifetime. My tongue circles around her center as I lap up her sweetness. Her legs start to tremble, and I finally take mercy, pulling her clit into my mouth, and sucking it gently, then harder when she starts to pant my name. Her hands grab my head and she curls over me as she comes with an explosion of heat on my tongue.

"Finn...Jesus," she gasps when she finally loosens her grip on my hair. I press a kiss to her inner thigh, caressing her hips until she slowly, with satisfyingly shaky legs, climbs off and stretches out beside me. I tug her right back into my side, unwilling to lose contact with her. My cock is pretty much screaming at me, desperate to plunge into Ashley and feel her lose control around me.

My focus is on trying to contain myself, and give her space to come down from the earth-shattering orgasm I just gave her. So much so that I miss her hand traveling down my body until it slides under my shorts and she wraps her fingers around me. I stiffen and fail at stifling my groan.

"Ashley. Don't do that unless you're ready for me," I growl. She presses a kiss to my shoulder and squeezes my dick gently at the same time.

"I'm so ready." Her hand slides lightly up and down my length, swirling at the top. She rises up, and makes quick work of pulling my shorts off. When she licks her lips at the sight of my cock, it just about does me in. She climbs back over my legs and leans down to kiss me. It's at that moment that I realize one crucial thing. When I had to relocate to the Airbnb, I had zero intention of hooking up here. Which means...

"Fuck. Ash, sweet girl, I don't have any condoms with me."

The speed with which she hops off the bed is impressive. "That's okay. I'll be right back."

Then, bare ass naked, which I certainly don't mind, Ashley runs out of the room and down the hall. When she returns, she's holding a baggie full of familiar packages. The clenching of my stomach bothers me. I shouldn't be jealous that she came to the island with condoms.

"You're prepared," I say, injecting a light teasing into the words that I really don't mean. Ashley climbs back on the bed only to slap my chest, rolling her eyes.

"They aren't mine, you dummy. They were in the toiletry kit in the bathroom."

I guess my surprise at that is evident because Ashley giggles.

"Yeah. Not what I was expecting, either, given the older lady who met me here when I checked in, but when she showed me the basket in the bathroom, she winked at me and told me to make sure I didn't take home a souvenir I didn't want."

"You're joking."

"Nope." Ashley pops the letter 'p' on that word, giving me a smirk as she opens the bag and takes several condoms out, dropping them on the bed beside us.

"Well, someone's optimistic." I raise my eyebrows at her. She arches one of her own before leaning down over my cock and taking it in her hands. A few quick strokes has me back to full strength, and I grab one of the packets and rip it open.

"You say optimistic, I say realistic." Ashley takes the condom from me and rolls it on, then swings her leg back over me once again. Goddamn, I can't wait until this damn knee is healed and I can fuck her properly.

"Come here, Ash." I cup her neck and draw her down. My cock is nestled between her legs. It might not be exactly where I want to be, but it feels pretty damn good. I kiss her, my tongue sliding in and out of her mouth. Her body softens against mine, the two of us melting together.

Her lips trail over to my ear. "Finn. You need to fuck me now," she whispers just before taking my earlobe in her teeth and biting down gently.

"God, yes."

My hands go to her hips and guide her up and over my cock. She reaches down between us and lines us up before sliding down my length achingly slowly. I reach up and cup her breasts, playing with her stiff nipples, earning a whimper of pleasure and a rush of sensation as she fits herself over me. Once she's fully seated, I let out a long breath. My hold on her hips tightens as she starts to rock back and forth. When she starts to lift up,

I want to hold her in place and not let her move, that's how intense this feeling of absolute rightness is, being connected to her like this. But then she slams back down on me, forcing a grunt out of me.

"Fuck, Ash. Ride me, sweet girl."

Her nails dig into my chest as she drops forward and rolls her hips. "Oh shit," she starts to moan, and her movements speed up slightly. I let go of her hips to tangle my hand in her hair, pulling her down while lifting my torso up at the same time so I can kiss her hard, swallowing the sounds of her desire.

She pulls back, but my hand is still in her hair, gripping it tight.

"Finn," she groans as her hands cup her breasts, then start to slide down. I intercept them with my own.

"That's my job, sweet girl," I growl before pinching her clit, earning a shriek.

"Yes, yes, yes, yes." She starts to lift up and slam down faster, alternating with a rock of her hips. My own are thrusting up to meet her every time and we lose ourselves in the motion. Bodies coming together, pulling just slightly apart, only to collide again, every time deeper and more powerful than the last. I'm consumed by Ashley, by the moment that's building between us. And when she starts to keen out my name, I know she's right there with me. She arches back, her hands falling to my thighs, and I keep one hand on her hip and the other is still playing with her clit, watching my cock ram in and out of her.

"Oh God, yes, there. Oh, holy fuck."

My orgasm is hurtling toward me and so is hers, but she's holding back. Don't ask me why, and don't ask me how I know, I just do.

"Let go, Ash. Come for me again."

With a scream of my name she does just that. Ashley flies off the edge into an orgasm even more spectacular than her first one, and I surrender to my own at the same moment.

She's ruined me.

Sex has never felt like this before, like two souls joining into one. Like there was no ending and no beginning, like we were suspended from reality for those minutes where we came together.

I should be terrified. But all I can think about is how desperately I want to do it again.

Chapter Eighteen

Ashley

That was…I don't even know how to describe it. I've had a few lovers, but never have I felt so thoroughly cherished, worshipped, and *possessed.* Finn took me to heights I never knew were possible, but for some crazy reason, this moment where we're tangled together, cuddling in that post-sex haze of happiness, feels just as amazing.

"Please tell me you don't have to work today," he mumbles against my head, pressing a kiss there. I love that he can't seem to stop touching me with his hands and his lips. It's as if now that the seal on our intimacy has been broken, he just can't get enough. We're opposite ends of a magnet, drawn together.

I shake my head. "I don't. I was going to check out a few secondhand shops in Westport that have new inventory, but it can wait."

Finn lifts up on one elbow, dislodging me from my comfortable pillow, aka, his chest. I pout, and he just kisses me with a grin. "Good. Then we don't have to get up yet." He takes on a mock serious expression. "I really should rest my knee after all."

A girlish giggle escapes me as I slap his chest. "What we just did doesn't really count as rest, though, does it?"

His eyes widen innocently. "It does when you're on top."

"Oh my God," I laugh, then shriek when he suddenly shifts onto his back, taking me with him so that once again I'm straddling his waist.

"Mmm. Yep, my knee feels better already just having you like this."

"You're ridiculous." I roll my eyes. But when he uses those amazing abs I can't stop touching to lift himself up so that he's sitting with his legs stretched out, all thoughts of teasing leave me. His cock is already hard again, and I can feel it pressing against me. He slides his hands down my legs and tugs them open so that they wrap around his waist.

"This is a new one for me," he comments suggestively, with a slight tilt of his hips that makes me gasp.

"Me too," I say as my head falls back. I'm overwhelmed with sensation, especially when he uses some sort of pelvic sorcery to swivel his hips, grinding his cock between my legs. Good God, I don't know how he's doing this with an injured leg, but I am most definitely not complaining.

And when it becomes almost too much, when I feel like I might spontaneously combust from unrequited desire, he reaches between us, covers himself, lines up and drives inside with a grunt of satisfaction.

"1, 2, 3, 4, I won the thumb war!" I pump my free hand triumphantly in the air as Finn's warm laugh rumbles out from him.

"You cheated."

"No way. There's no rule against distracting your opponent in a thumb war," I protest, batting my eyelashes at him with an impish smile.

"Whose idea was it to have naked thumb wars, anyway?" he grumbles good naturedly, wrapping his arms around me tightly. I nestle my head back down on his chest, content in our warm cocoon. The musky smell of our lovemaking lingers in the air. We probably should get up and shower, but the last two hours have been heavenly. Just then, my stomach lets out an embarrassing rumble.

"Sorry," I say sheepishly, but Finn just dislodges me and sits up, running his hands through his thick hair. Seriously, it should be illegal for a man to have luscious hair like he does.

"Nah, we should eat." He turns back to me, and the shy smile he gives me is so at odds with the confident, sexy, dominant side he has in bed. "But maybe we could just order pizza and stay here today?"

I sit up to meet him, and kiss his shoulder. "Deal. How do you feel about watching a movie? There's a DVD of the original

Chucky movie out in the main room, and I could totally go for some old school horror."

"Oh. Umm, could we maybe choose something else?" He clears his throat, and the tips of his ears are turning red.

I take his head in my hands and turn him to face me, taking in the blush on his stubbled cheeks. Cue my heart melting into a puddle of goo. "You don't like scary movies?"

Finn whips his head back and forth. "Not at all." He visible shudders. "I got totally creeped out by watching *The Shining* when I was a teenager, and ever since then, I just can't."

My amusement at this vulnerability must not be as well hidden as I thought because his eyes narrow, and Finn pokes at my bare side. "Don't laugh, woman."

A giggle sneaks past my lips. "Sorry."

"Now you've done it," he mock growls before his hands come to my waist and he starts to tickle. I shriek in surprise and we fall back on the bed in a tangle of laughter.

Eventually, we manage to get dressed — well, if loose shorts for Finn and one of his T-shirts for me counts as dressed. We order pizza, I grab some cut up veggies I had in the fridge, and we picnic on his bed. Finn is merciless in teasing me about my hot sauce addiction, watching in horror as I pour it all over my slice of pizza.

"You try going to an all-girls school that served the blandest food ever for lunch and tell me you wouldn't fall in love with hot sauce the second you had freedom over your lunches," I say in all seriousness, licking a drop of hot sauce off my finger. When I go to put the next sauce-covered finger in my mouth, Finn grabs it and brings it to his mouth, sucking it off in a way that would make my panties wet. If I were wearing any.

And that's how round three of the BSE — best sex ever — starts. Is there a better way to spend a wet, wintery day? I don't think so.

All good things must come to an end, however, and the next morning I wake up feeling no small amount of dread as the idea of facing reality sets in. Both Finn and I have to go to the winery today, and we haven't talked about what that'll be like. Will whatever this is between us exist outside the bubble of our Airbnb?

He gives me a sweet kiss when I leave his room to go and get dressed in my own. We've already agreed to drive together, seeing as Finn can't exactly bend his knee very well right now. That will make sense to anyone who might see us. But will he hold my hand, will he touch me, in front of other people? Or will he go back to being the man who keeps me at arm's length? I still have yet to figure out why that is, and as I stand in the bathroom brushing my teeth, I ponder that question. Thinking back, the signs of our mutual attraction have been glaringly obvious since the second I bumped into him my first day in Dogwood Cove. But he has switched from hot and cold around me so often, my head spins. I want to believe things are different now, that we've moved past the indecisiveness and solidly into some sort of undefined relationship, but what if I'm wrong?

My nerves and uncertainty hovers around me the entire drive to the winery, not diminished at all by the fact that Finn is holding my hand, and his thumb is stroking my knuckles. He doesn't say anything, just looks out the window as we make the short trip. I can only assume he's caught up in his own thoughts just as much as I am.

When we get to the winery, he gives my hand one final squeeze and at last peeks over at me with a brief smile. "I'll see you in a bit, yeah?"

I nod. Should we hug? Do I lean in for a kiss? Apparently, the answer to both questions is *no* as Finn climbs out of my car and limps slowly toward the barn that houses his equipment. I tried to convince him to take his crutches, but he just scoffed and said he was fine. *Men.*

His dismissive departure rattles me slightly, but I try to rationalize it. We're putting on a professional front at work. Okay, I can do this. I pull on my toque and gloves, get out of my car, and make my way through the cold to the tasting room. Once I'm inside, I peel off my winter wear and look around in satisfaction. The room is coming together just as I imagined. It's warm, inviting, eclectic, and decadent all at once. It's a space that says, "Come in, have a drink, stay a while." Which is exactly what I wanted.

"It is lovely, Ashley." Pierre's admiring voice reaches me and I turn to meet him with a smile.

"Thank you."

The door to the outside opens and Finn hobbles in. Pierre rushes over to him instantly. "What are you doing walking around like that? You'll do more damage, you fool." He grabs Finn's arm and helps him over to one of the chairs that still has plastic covering the cushion. Finn sinks down on it and turns to Pierre with a grateful smile.

"I'm fine, but thanks."

Fine? He's fine? Well, I'm not. He hasn't even *glanced* at me yet. And now he's deep in conversation with Pierre about some gadget he wants for blending, and I can't ignore the hurt blossoming inside. There's keeping things professional, and then there's ignoring the woman you had sex with multiple times last night. And what he's doing, is definitely the latter. Honestly, it's cheapening everything we shared, and making me feel like all he did was take advantage of my proximity the other night.

As I stew in my own thoughts, pain and anger building inside my heart, Finn gets up, and with a final word to Pierre, he leaves. All without saying a single word to me.

That's enough to send me over the edge. The past thirty-six hours meant something to me, and now I find myself questioning if they meant anything to him. They were amazing, and I felt connected to him in a way I never have before. So this man, this man who won't give me the time of day just because we aren't holed up in a bedroom somewhere, this man needs to get lost. I'm confused, I'm hurt, and I'm mad.

"Excuse me, Pierre, I forgot something in my car."

I grab my toque and slam it on my head, leaving my jacket behind and I head outside, not waiting for his reply. A quick glance around doesn't reveal where Finn has gone, so I head to the barn that houses his tanks and blending room, but the door is locked. *Where is he?*

I walk around the barn toward the fields that slope down to a small lake that is part of the next property over. Even as my mind swirls with confusion and annoyance toward Finn, the design part of me never stops. I could see landscaping this area into a perfect picnic spot for guests, maybe even the occasional wedding.

I find the man in question standing on the edge of the hillside, staring out. Part of me wants to get angry at his stupid decision to limp out here on the uneven ground, but I'm so frustrated. If he wants to be an idiot, he can just go right ahead and do that.

"What the hell is going on?"

He turns at my voice, and I take in the play of emotions over his face. Hurt, guilt, defensiveness and confusion all meld together. Whatever's going on inside his head, it can't be easy on him, and that right there softens my anger. I still want an explanation, but I'm not feeling as if I was used for sex like I was starting to back in the tasting room.

"Look, Finn, maybe you don't realize this, but fucking a woman and then ignoring her the next day isn't cool. Like, at all. Which means there had better be a reason you keep going back and forth around me. I'm trying really hard to believe that, because if there *isn't*, then you're just an ass who's playing with my emotions. And my ability to judge people's intentions is usually pretty good, and that's not what I was feeling last night."

The stricken expression he gives me is all the evidence I need to know I'm right. There is a reason, he's not just being a jerk.

"Just tell me, Finn," I say quietly.

He inhales slowly and I wait patiently. Whatever he's going to say doesn't scare me. If anything, I feel a sense of relief that he's finally going to open up to me.

"Her name was Cassandra. She was a server at the winery I worked at down in Napa a few years ago." He names some fancy-sounding place I've never heard of, but I nod all the same. "Little did I know, her uncle owned the damn place. We hooked up; I thought we were on the same page."

Finn turns away from me, running his fingers through his hair. He seems nervous, ashamed even when he looks back at me. "I knew I didn't want to stay in California forever, so I didn't want anything serious. But I guess she didn't believe me. When I tried to clarify that with her, she got upset. Said I had led her on, fooled her. I didn't, I swear." His eyes are pleading with me to believe him, so I place my hand on his arm and slide it down so I can take his hand. He squeezes mine tightly. "Anyway, to make a long story short, she complained to her uncle, who sided with her and let me go. His reasoning was that he didn't want any tension or awkward feelings amongst staff." His gaze drops down to our hands, then back up to meet mine, and the worry I see there makes me want to wrap him in my arms. "After that, I swore to never date someone I worked with. Losing that job wasn't a huge deal, but the realization that it *could* have been so much worse was sobering. Making wine is my passion, it's the one thing I've always known I want to do. And now, this winery, this is the culmination of all my work, all my dreams come true. And I'm fucking terrified to do anything that might jeopardize that. You're important to Pierre, and I don't know how he'll feel about us sleeping together."

I want to ask why the heck Pierre has to know, and even if he did know, why that needs to matter in the slightest, but I don't. Because the dejected tone in his voice tells me he's expecting my rejection, my anger. And truthfully, it's still there. The fact is, it hurts that he equates what we shared to some fling with a server in his past. Then again, I guess maybe to him, that's all it was. A fling. Two people giving in to chemistry. The possibility that he's worried I would do or say anything that could harm his future, his career, is insane. But I guess he doesn't know that. I guess he doesn't know me well enough to know I would never do something so cruel. One thing bothers me more than anything else. It's the one question I need to ask, no matter how painful the answer may be.

"Do you regret sleeping with me?"

His eyes widen in horror. "God, no, Ash." His hands find my hips and he pulls me closer. "I'm sorry, sweet girl. I know I'm screwing things up, the truth is, I have no clue how to handle things between us. But I definitely do not regret a single second of what we did. How could I, when every second with you was absolute perfection." His words ring with honesty, and when I lift my eyes to his face, the worry that was there before is intensified. I bring one hand up to cup his cheek and give him a small smile.

"Good."

One word is all it takes for the tension to leave his body. His head sags forward to meet mine.

"The truth is, you're making me feel things I've never felt. Want things I never thought I would want. These...feelings...they confuse the fuck out of me. But they also excite me, Ash. Sleeping with you, waking up with you in my arms, hell, watching you drown perfectly good pizza in hot sauce made me so damn happy. I'm almost grateful I injured my knee because apparently half-stoned-on-painkillers Finn is brave enough to do things sober Finn isn't." He grins, and I choke back a laugh, feeling wetness pool in my eyes. I don't know what I was expecting when I came to confront Finn about his behaviour, but it wasn't this romantic, heartfelt, outpouring of words. Truthfully, they scare me a bit. Because I don't know if I'm ready for this, whatever this is.

He leans in to kiss me and my eyes flutter closed in anticipation. "I want this, Ashley. I want you. I want us. Never doubt that."

"There you two are!"

Pierre's voice pierces the moment and I startle, pulling back in surprise and no small amount of disappointment. But Finn keeps a hold of me as we turn to face his partner, my father's friend. This is Finn's worst nightmare, I'm guessing. He's so worried about what Pierre would think that I was ready to tell him I was okay with keeping things a secret for now. But that ship has clearly sailed, so instead, my stomach churns with dread, waiting to hear Pierre's reaction to finding us lip-locked in the field.

"I was looking for you two, I wanted to make sure all was well, but I can see it is." He smiles, and his eyes drop down to our joined hands. "I'm heading home for tonight. Finn, that part you want should be here tomorrow. I paid for express shipping."

"Thank you," Finn manages to get out the words, but his voice is strained, and judging from the vice grip he has on me, he's nervous to see if Pierre says anything else about catching us in an obviously intimate moment. But he's not letting go, and that has to mean something, right?

Pierre makes to leave, but pauses and turns back to face us. He waves his hands at us in an encompassing gesture. "This is good."

That's all he says before he pivots on his foot and walks back to the parking lot.

"I...did he just...I'm confused," I stammer out, tilting my head to one side. Finn's low chuckle envelops me at the same time his arms wrap around my waist.

"That was Pierre taking care of any concerns or worries either of us might have about how he feels. Apparently, our mixing business with pleasure isn't an issue with him."

I can hear the relief in his words, and I let it seep into me. I slowly twist around so that I'm facing him and grab the ends of his scarf. "Does that mean no more distant Finn?"

He bends down and kisses my neck in response. "Babe, I'm going to stay so close to you, you'll get sick of me."

Not likely. I'm starting to think I'll never have enough of Finn McNeil.

Chapter Nineteen

Finn

Spending the first week of this new stage of our relationship with me limping around, unable to bear weight directly on my knee, is not exactly how I would choose to build a connection with Ashley. I've been in a few somewhat serious relationships before, and the best part about the beginning is the passion.

Don't get me wrong, lazing around in bed is fucking awesome, and our compatibility in the bedroom is incredible. But I want to take her out on dates where she doesn't have to drive, I want to sweep her off her feet, hell, I want to be able to go down on her in the shower like she did to me yesterday. God, just thinking about it has me hard again. It's becoming a permanent issue. All it takes is one whiff of her perfume, delicate and bright, like a spring morning mixed with a hint of citrus, and I'm weak. Her smile makes me feel warm inside, her touch makes me want to go caveman and trap her in bed for a week.

But she deserves more than just a horny guy who can't even put in his best effort in bed. Which is why I coughed up the money for a hotel tonight, told her to pack an overnight bag, and had her drive us to Victoria. I'm determined to show her a good time, even if it has to be modified for my fucking knee.

"Are you going to tell me what we're doing?" she asks, sounding amused and extremely curious.

"I already told you — no. Can't a guy surprise a girl with a night out?" I tease, moving my hand to the top of her thigh and rubbing it back and forth. "Just relax and enjoy."

She lets out an adorable huff. "I am relaxed. This is me relaxed."

That makes me snort under my breath. "Really. So your obsessive packing, constant badgering me about directions, and the twenty questions you've already asked on the drive is your idea of relaxed?"

"I'm curious, okay?" she says, exasperation evident. I chuckle and squeeze her thigh in response.

"Don't worry about it. I just want to say thank you for taking care of me after my fall."

Her eyes dart over to meet mine as we pull to a stop at a traffic light. "Finn, you wouldn't have been injured if it wasn't for me. Taking care of you is the least I could do."

My hand cups her chin, even as I keep one eye out for when the light turns green. "Ash, stop feeling guilty. This isn't your fault."

She turns her gaze back to the road, but I see a small smile dance across her lips.

"Besides, if you hadn't been such a sexy nurse, who knows if we would have ever gotten over ourselves enough to discover how fucking hot we are together in bed." I punctuate my words with a slide of my hand up her thigh to lightly run up the crease of her hip, running close enough to tease her but not distract her.

"Finn..." She bites her lip and darts her gaze over to me.

"Mmm. We might need to check out the hotel room before we go out tonight," I mutter under my breath, bringing my hands back to my lap. I'm not sure I can control myself right now. Ashley's sweet giggle is sweet music to my ears.

When we pull up to the hotel, we climb out of the car. Well, I hate to admit it, but Ashley has to get out by herself, walk around, and get my crutches out of the back to hand them to me. Thankfully, a valet comes over quickly to unload our bags and carry them inside. I'm not sure how my pride would handle Ash having to carry them all inside for us.

When we reach our room, I'm nervous about what she'll think. She comes from money and is probably used to much fancier places than this. But the excitement is shining from her when she walks over and wraps her arms around my waist.

"Careful, you're hugging me," I tease and she slaps my ass.

"Oh hush, you're huggable."

"High praise. I'll take it." I kiss the top of her head. "We've got an hour or so before we have to go out, what do you want to do? There's a hot tub downstairs, or we could watch a movie, or..."

Her head tilts up and her eyes are hooded with desire. "I choose *or*…"

"Good choice," I growl. Then, letting my crutches fall away, I push her down on the bed and show her exactly how I want to pass the time.

Part one of the evening I have planned involves dinner at a tiny bistro tucked away on a side street in the heart of downtown. It's the kind of place you could drive past and never realize was there unless you knew about it. Their specialty is seafood, fresh from the boats that bring it into the harbour. I had a moment of panic when I realized I had no clue if Ashley even liked seafood, but the way her eyes lit up and her exclamations of interest as we read the menu reassured me quickly.

Over a shared starter of a steamer pot filled with seafood, and a bottle of Sauvignon blanc, we swapped childhood stories.

"Hold on, hold on. You're telling me you spent an entire *month* in Spain as part of your Spanish class in high school?"

She has the decency to blush, and nibble on her lower lip. I reach over and smooth my thumb over her mouth, freeing it.

"I know I was privileged. But private school wasn't all good, trust me," she says drily.

"The princess nickname?" I ask quietly and she nods quickly. "I'm sorry I ever hurt you by saying that."

"No, Finn, you didn't know. It's fine." She smiles, and takes a sip of her wine. "Besides." She lifts her shoulders up delicately. "I kind of was spoiled. In the best possible way. My dad is everything to me. I don't remember my mother, she passed away when I was very young. So my father has been the only parent I've ever known. We're incredibly close. He's the reason I went to university here, and started my company in Vancouver. I didn't want to move away from him."

A dull thud echoes inside my mind at that statement. It doesn't bode well for us and any future we might have together. Resolutely, I push that away and focus on the here and now. I've got more planned for our weekend, and I hope she loves it.

"Finn, this is incredible," Ashley's voice is full of wonder as she clutches my hand under the fleece blanket draped over our legs. We're in a horse-drawn carriage, taking us along the streets of Victoria. There's enough snow on the ground combined with the twinkling lights in the trees and lining the legislature building that it feels like a winter wonderland. Something out of a movie, even. I have to admit, it's insanely romantic, far more than any other date I've been on. And the best part is, I'm off my feet, so it's as if my knee isn't even a problem. We're cuddled up under a blanket, with some soft instrumental Christmas music playing and a thermos of hot chocolate. The driver is taking us on some long, windy route, and the views are spectacular.

"I've never been on a carriage ride," I admit, smiling down at her. "But this is amazing."

She sighs and rests her head on my shoulder. "It really is. Good job on the date planning."

I tilt my chin so I can kiss her. I've found she always squeezes me just a little bit tighter if I kiss the top of her head. So I try to do it a lot.

We roll along in the dark, waving back at pedestrians who wave at us, smiling at the kids who are excited to see the horse. When one little girl calls out, "Look, Mommy, a prince and a princess!" Ashley buries her head in my shoulder to stifle her laughter while I smile gamely at the child.

"Well, that was ironic," I snicker under my breath and Ashley lightly slaps my arm as she holds back her own laugh.

An hour later, we're back in her car, driving to the hotel. When we get inside, and we're in the elevator, I lean against the back wall and take a deep, satisfying breath. Tonight has gone perfectly.

"So, it's Friday," Ashley starts conversationally. I give her a side-eyed glance, not sure where she's going with this.

"Yeah, it is."

"Wanna watch *Friday the 13th*?" She lets out a devilish giggle and then squirms away when my fingers go to tickle her side.

"No, you horrible woman, I don't."

"But I promise we can sleep with the light on, and I'll hold your hand if you get scared," she teases in a singsong voice, dancing away from me.

"Get back here, you," I joke, poking her with my crutch. The elevator doors open on our floor and she walks backward out into the hall, shaking her head. I follow as quickly as I can, cursing my damn knee every step that takes her farther from me.

At the door to our room, I trap her at last, my hands coming to either side of her shoulders, pinning her in place. My lips find a spot of bare skin on her neck, and I whisper a kiss there.

"You shouldn't torment me like that."

"Why not?" she says breathily, tilting her head to give me more access. "I think it's adorable you won't watch scary movies."

I take the key card out of my wallet and slide it in, opening the door. My other arm is wrapped around her waist, holding her to me, and I'm somehow managing to keep the damn crutches under my armpits.

"If you want to spend tonight with my eyes closed while you watch a movie, fine. But I was thinking I'd rather make use of that large jacuzzi tub."

I feel her sharp intake of breath under my arm and I wrap it tighter around her, pulling her flush with my groin where I know she can feel my dick hardening.

"That's a better idea," she murmurs.

"I thought so, too."

In the room, I head straight to the bathroom, turn the lights on low using the dimmer switch, and start to fill the tub. I grab the container of bath salts the hotel provided, open it, and give it a sniff. It's musky, with an underlying aroma of jasmine. Nice. I dump them in, check the temperature, then once I'm satisfied,

I hobble my way into the bedroom to find Ashley with her back to me in nothing but her bra and panties.

"Fuck, babe," I sigh, going over to her. My hands run from her shoulders, down her sides, landing on her lace covered hips. From there I trail up her spine, unclasp her bra, and slide it off her shoulders. She turns to the side slightly.

"You're way too overdressed." She turns in my arms fully, tempting me with her perfect breasts. But I don't get the chance to enjoy them before she's lifting my sweater over my head, her nails lightly scratching down my bare torso. "Turn," she directs me in a soft voice, and I pivot on my good leg until I can sit on the edge of the bed. She drops to her knees between my legs, like every man's wet dream come to life. My pants are undone, and I lift my hips so she can slide them off, freeing my cock. When she licks her lips and looks up at me with those large, hooded eyes, I stop her.

"No, sweet girl. Tonight is about you."

Carefully, I stand up, leave the crutches where they are, and lead her into the bathroom. I shut off the taps, then face Ashley and slide her panties down her legs so that we're both naked. I slowly get into the tub, feeling my good leg shake with the effort of supporting most of my body weight as I lower down. But it's worth it when the warm water washes over me, and Ashley climbs in and settles between my legs.

We lay there for a few minutes, our fingers tangling together and lightly splashing the water. Her head is resting on my shoulder, and I'd be lying if I said I didn't want this moment, this feeling, to last forever. Then Ashley shifts, and her ass, nestled against my cock, brings a small groan from my lips. She giggles, the tease, which means payback.

I free one hand from hers, and let it drift below the water, drawing slow, lazy lines up and down her stomach, starting between her breasts and running to just below her belly button. With each pass, I let the whorls I'm tracing draw closer and closer to her core, but always stopping just before I reach there. Soon her hips start to lift, straining to meet my touch, and I pull her earlobe between my teeth.

"Nope, I'm in control now, babe." I kiss everywhere my lips can reach and wrap my other arm across her chest, letting my hand tease and tug on her nipple. Her hands come up and twist around my neck.

"Finn, please," she says pleadingly.

I suck gently where her neck slopes to meet her shoulder and she moans softly. Painstakingly slow, I drag my fingers through the water, down her stomach, down her leg, back up and down the other leg, until finally, I slide in between them to stroke up her seam. Her hips lift, seeking more contact, and it's all I can do not to give it to her immediately. But I want to draw this out. My fingers slip over her folds, circling around her entrance.

"You're torturing me," she groans.

"Mmm. No, I'm pleasuring you," I rasp in her ear, just as I plunge one finger into her heat, sending water sloshing everywhere. She cries out my name, her fingers tightening in the hair at the base of my neck until it's a heady mix of pain and pleasure. The steam in the air, the dim lights, and her voice echoing around us, it's a feast for all of my senses, and I'm lost to it.

I add a second finger, and bring my palm to her clit, rubbing in circles as I twist my fingers to stroke her inner walls. I can tell I find her G-spot when her toes curl against the end of the tub and her cries turn to moans. My cock is rock hard, and her every movement is the best kind of torture as she rubs against me. I love how wild and free she is when she gives herself over to what I'm doing. And when she lets go, it's almost enough to send me over the edge as well, just watching her.

I could get used to this woman.

CHAPTER TWENTY

Ashley

After Victoria, I was flying high for over a day. I felt closer to Finn after just over a week of dating than I did with Tyson after six months of dating, hell, even after a year of being together. It's overwhelming, exciting, and confusing. Because at the end of the day, there's a deadline looming. In another month, maybe less, the tasting room will be finished, and I'll be...well, that's the question. What will I do when this job is done? I still don't have anything else lined up on the mainland, but I haven't exactly spent much time looking for clients, either. Tom's offer to work with him over here *has* been on my mind a lot. I love it on the island. I love the slower pace, I love the friendly people, I love the community. I love walking into The Nutty Muffin and being greeted by name, not just by the staff, but by some of the locals who recognize me. I love the small grocery store, with its single cash register, and the old couple who run it. I love the gazebo in the center of town, where kids play, and sometimes musicians set up to serenade everyone.

I love everything about this town. But my dad is on the mainland. Never once have I considered moving far away from him. And okay, Dogwood Cove isn't *that* far, but a two hour ferry ride isn't something to dismiss.

My relationship with Finn adds a layer of complexity to it. Every time I go to talk to him, ask him where he sees things going, I panic. It's too much, too fast. I can't stay here. He doesn't want anything serious. All the excuses, some real, some probably not, fly through my brain at a million miles an hour and I freeze.

Tonight we're all back at Hastings again. But this time, it's different. Finn isn't at the other end of the table scowling at me. He's beside me, his arm wrapped around my shoulders and his thumb drawing circles on the side of my arm. Also, this time the bar owner Dean and his wife Riley have joined our group. Riley's a beautiful woman, full of vibrancy, and all glowy and happy with the cutest little baby bump that she can't stop rubbing. Mila filled me in on how Jackson freaked out one day, thinking Mila was buying pregnancy tests for herself. In actuality, she was picking them up for Riley when Riley's car, which has special hand controls for her to use, was in the shop. Riley came over in her wheelchair just as Mila was telling me this, and the two women hugged, showing just how close they are.

"I've heard all about the tasting room you're working on," Riley says with excitement. "I can't wait until this baby is born and I can visit the winery!"

Finn leans in front of me and gives her a smile. "I'll make sure to have a special bottle chilling for your first time."

"Hey, Prince Charming, quit hitting on my wife," Dean calls out as he walks to the table with two pitchers of beer and I face Finn with a raised eyebrow.

"Prince Charming?"

Finn shakes his head and laughs. "Yeah, only Dean calls me that. All because of one time —" he raises his voice so Dean can hear "— one fucking time I hit on a woman in the bar."

"And she shot you down!" Everyone starts to laugh and I pat Finn's cheek and smirk.

"Her loss, my gain."

Good Lord, the smoulder he gives me is so damn hot I want to check to make sure my panties aren't on fire. They aren't...but they are damp. He kisses me, a long, slow, deep kiss that only ends when someone catcalls from the other end of the table. When we separate, I'm blushing. Finn strokes my cheek and presses one more quick kiss to my lips before turning back to the table and taking a drink of his beer.

"Okay, okay, enough you idiots."

"Ashley, have you ever been snowshoeing?" Summer asks from across the table.

"Yeah, a few times I went up the coast mountains with some friends, and last year my best friend Sarah and I did a trek out in Manning Park. Why?" I reply.

"There are some amazing trails up Mount Washington. When Finn's knee is healed, we should plan a trip."

"I'd love that. There's something about walking through a fresh snowfall with no one around. It's incredible."

Finn leans over to whisper in my ear, "You know what would make that even better? If there was a cabin at the end of the trail, and I could peel off each layer of your clothing until you were bare. Then it would be just me, you, and a bottle of wine I would lick off your skin."

Electricity runs up and down my spine, and I shift in my seat to try and ease the arousal his words and that fantasy ignite inside of me.

He kisses my neck, and I have to bite the inside of my cheek to stop from moaning. I've never been this openly intimate and affectionate with a man in public before, and the allure of Finn is making it hard to resist.

"Someday we'll make that happen, sweet girl," he says quietly. I can't look at him right now, especially not after he calls me sweet girl. It turns my insides to mush, and I'm not entirely certain I'll be able to stop myself from climbing into his lap right here, in front of everyone.

A little while later I get up to use the ladies room. When I come out, I find Mila, Riley, Summer, and Serena waiting for me. Only Paige and Abby are missing.

"Umm, hi guys," I say cautiously. They're all smiling, but it's still strange.

"Hi. So. You and Finn. This is amazing!" Summer claps her hands together excitedly, but Mila reaches over and shushes her.

"Stop, Summer, don't freak her out."

"Freak me out how?"

"We're really excited you guys are together now, that's all," Riley chimes in, her eyes dancing.

I arch my brow at them and fold my arms across my chest. "And this required all of you to ambush me outside of the bathroom *why*?"

"Because the last time we talked about you and Finn, you were pretty set on there *not* being anything between you. Clearly, that's changed and this is the first chance we've had to talk about it," Serena states, as if it should be obvious.

I guess I'm not used to this kind of oversharing. Sarah and I talk a lot, but I've never had a group of friends like this, who all know each other's business so intimately. It's strange, but not entirely unwelcome.

"Look, I'm not going into details, but yes, things changed. He finally showed me the side that you guys see."

Mila claps her hands to her heart and pretends to swoon. "Aww. Our boy swept you off your feet?"

"Hard to do when he's on crutches, but yeah." I grin.

"Wait. Does this mean you're thinking about staying in town after the tasting room is done?" Summer asks eagerly, and all of the women have similar hopeful expressions on their faces.

My eyes cast down to the floor. "I...I don't know, you guys. There's a lot to consider. It's a big decision, and I really don't want to make it based on a week of good sex."

"Of course. That's totally valid," Mila says quickly. "We're just really hoping that the more reasons we give you to stay, the better the chance is that you will. And good sex is a good reason, isn't it?"

I have to laugh at that. "Yeah, it is. But it's not the deciding factor."

"Got it. Okay, had better space out our return to the table so the guys don't suspect anything. Who knows if Paige and Abby kept them distracted enough," Serena says.

"You really think they don't know we came back here to talk to Ashley?" Summer remarks wryly, and they all giggle.

When we get back to the table, Reid is the first one to pipe up. "Have a good gossip, ladies?"

I snicker as Abby elbows him. "You weren't meant to notice, babe!"

"Oh, come on, like it wasn't obvious they were going to find Ashley and bug her for details."

"Even if we did do that, and I'm not saying we did, but it's none of your business," Mila announces as she sits down on Jackson's lap. I watch her open affection with him, and with everyone, with a smile as I take my seat next to Finn.

"Did they interrogate you about us?" he asks quietly, his hand coming to cover mine on my leg.

"Yeah, but don't worry. I didn't tell them about your fear of horror movies." I pat his cheek and grin to ease the sting of my teasing.

"You're evil."

"You like it," I reply saucily.

His gaze softens. "I do."

I don't let myself think too much about what I see written on his face when he says that.

I can't.

Because I'm not ready for the answering emotions it stirs in my own heart.

Chapter Twenty-One

Finn

I never in a million years imagined being in a relationship again at this point in my life. I figured the next few years would be solely focused on the winery with the occasional trip to Victoria when I needed some companionship of the female kind. And yes, I realize that makes me sound like a total douchebag. But I honestly didn't plan on having the time to date, or the desire to put any effort into a relationship.

Yet, here I am, finding myself growing more and more attracted to Ashley with every passing day. How I ever thought she would be a thorn in my side, or more of a hassle than anything else, I don't know. Her ideas are innovative, creative, and best of all, cost efficient.

And that's just at work.

At home, or at least our temporary home, it's even better. Our chemistry is off the charts. I've found myself laughing and having more fun with her than I've ever had with a woman who isn't just a friend. I'm slowly letting myself believe I can truly have it all.

She hasn't spent a night in "her" bedroom since that first night, and slowly her clothes are mixing with mine in the closet of my room. We're together all day, every day, which could feel suffocating this early on, but instead it just feels normal. As if this is the way it was always meant to be, and the frustration and confusion we both were feeling before we gave in to our attraction was fate's way of telling us to get it together and accept the inevitable.

She was meant for me.

She's unleashed a side of me I didn't really know existed, a side that thinks of romantic date nights, and that's fixated on feelings and emotions, not just the physical chemistry. Unfortunately, along with the good comes the potentially bad. I can't seem to accept the lack of certainty over her future. What happens when the tasting room is done? Will she stay, or is she headed back to the city? We seem to have come to an unspoken agreement not to talk about that yet, as if we both know what we have is too new, too fragile, to face that conversation. But it has to happen, and soon. Because I've started thinking ahead to things I want to do with her in the spring and summer. I can see her walking with me through the vines, caring for the grapes, having a picnic with one of the first bottles of wine I'll make here.

I go to see the doctor this afternoon, hopefully to get cleared to walk and drive, and generally be normal again. It's been three weeks since I fell and that's three weeks too long of being dependent on others for so much of what I need. But first, I have to get through lunch over burgers at Hastings with my best friend, who is determined to call me out on my hesitation in talking to Ashley.

"Finding out you've got a heart capable of feeling things is good, dude. Whoever first decided that guys don't get to be in touch with their emotions was full of shit."

I watch Ethan take a huge bite of his burger, searching for any hint of teasing in his face, but it's not there. He really does mean that. And he's not wrong.

"All I'm saying is, embrace it. You've spent your entire adulthood avoiding commitments with women, and that's fine. But now you've found one who's worth changing for."

"I haven't *completely* avoided commitment," I reply half-heartedly. "There was Tessa in college, remember? We dated for a couple months."

"Right. A couple months. Did you at any point think about the future with her or were you fixated on the present?"

"Jesus. Summer's turned you into a fucking therapist," I mutter, but there's no malice behind the words. Ethan's always had a softer side, a part of him capable of feeling things in a way I never was. I'd never admit it to him, but it's something I've always admired. "And I dated your sister, remember? I treated her well." I smirk at him, and Ethan rolls his eyes in return.

"Don't mention my sister. That's a period in time I want to forget. And this isn't all because of Summer." Ethan pauses, takes a sip of his beer, then continues. "Okay, it's mostly because of her. But it's also my parents, Mila and Jackson, and Reid and Abby. Love isn't something to run away from. It makes life better."

"Hey, I didn't say anything about love."

"I know you didn't. But I also know you're probably holding back with Ashley. Waiting for the other shoe to drop. What if it doesn't have to? Can you let yourself just be happy?"

I let my head nod in response as his words sink in. I don't really have any reason for my lack of experience in a committed relationship. I grew up with two loving parents, a great example of true love and partnership. They worked through the hard times as a team, and never shied away from showing affection in front of me. Deep inside I've always wanted that, but for some reason I've pushed that desire aside until now. It would be easy to chalk it all up to timing, or fate, and maybe that's true. Or maybe Ethan's right, and it's because of Ashley.

"Moving on, I've got some good news. You can move back into your house next week. The landlord and I finalized the repair plan, and it should be done on the weekend. No more missing roof, no more Airbnb."

I try to muster up the gratitude and excitement I'm guessing Ethan is expecting, but all I can manage is a half-assed smile. "Cool. Thanks."

He keeps on talking, something about the Vancouver hockey team's shot at playoffs, I think. I'm not really paying attention anymore. He doesn't push me to comment, and thank fuck for that because I honestly don't know how to put into words what the news about the house does to me. I know I should feel relief that in less than a week I can move home, but the truth is, that house doesn't feel like home. It doesn't have anything of me in it except my clothes and a few personal items. It was a place I could go to sleep, and that's basically it. The Airbnb served the exact same purpose, with the added bonus of Ashley being there.

If I go back to my rental house, where does that leave us? It's not like I can ask her to move in with me; even with our unconventional beginning, I know that would be too much, too soon. But if I move out of the Airbnb, will she see that as me pulling away, going back to the mixed messages I was guilty of sending her in the beginning? Not to mention that the very thought of not spending every night with her in my arms physically hurts. And that pain is amplified by the idea of her being hours away on the mainland. If I knew she was staying in Dogwood Cove, it would be easier. I wouldn't have this growing doubt that everything is going to change, and not in a good way.

It's a little embarrassing that it takes so long for me to reach the inevitable conclusion. I need to man up and just talk to her.

The idea of talking to Ashley about her plans is one thing. Executing it is another. Thankfully, my visit to the doctor leads to good news. I don't have to use crutches any longer, I can drive, and return to normal activities within the limits of my pain. I walk from the doctor's office back to the Airbnb where my car is parked, and take the time to come up with a way to finally give Ashley the romance she deserves. And if it happens to set the scene for us to talk about the future, all the better.

At the Airbnb I jump in the shower, take the time to style my hair, trim my beard, and for the first time in months, get dressed in clothes I haven't had any reason to wear lately. Crisp charcoal grey dress pants and a white button-down shirt. After going back and forth in my head over the idea, I took the chance and called Pierre. I needed to make sure I'd have some privacy with Ashley for what I have in mind. He was all too happy to assure me that he'd be long gone before I arrive, but that Ashley had already told him her plans to stay behind and hang some artwork. My partner tried to warn me about treating Ashley well, but in the end he couldn't hide his happiness that we were together. Looking back, I don't even know why I ever thought he wouldn't approve of our dating. The man loves love.

After making a couple of necessary stops, I head out to the winery. When I get there, I bypass the building where my girl is hard at work, and drive straight around to park in front of the barn. Hopping out of my car, I walk around to the trunk and grab the blankets and pillows I took from the Airbnb, and the bag that holds the few décor items from my rental house that I thought might help my plan along. Candles and wine glasses being the most important. And of course, I have a cooler bag that holds the crucial ingredient — wine.

Unlocking the door to the barn, I flick on some of the lights. The steel tanks don't exactly lend themselves to a romantic atmosphere, but this isn't my final destination. Out the back side of the barn is the half underground cellar we had built that will hold our barrels for aging, and racks of bottles when the wine is ready for that stage. I may be biased, but I think the cellar is stunning inside. We modeled it after the cellars found in the wineries in the Okanagan and down in Napa, with exposed beam ceilings, wooden floors and walls, and warm lighting. With a long table in the middle where we can provide tastings, intricate temperature controls, and room for all the barrels and bottles we could possibly want it to contain, this space is my nirvana. The barn, with its steel tanks and blending room, is where my work will take place. But here, this is where the magic takes place. And this is where I want to set things up for Ashley.

There's no furniture except a long table, and most of the racks are empty, but that doesn't detract from the intimate vibe of the dimly lit room. I set up the candles I've got, but I don't light them yet. The blankets get laid out on the floor, with pillows piled on top. The floor is hard, but hopefully I've managed to make it comfortable enough. Once I've got our seating area arranged the best I can, I stand up and start to line up the bottles of wine I brought, opening the merlot to let it breathe. A quick dash up the stairs to grab a stool and finally, I light the candles, then survey my setup with satisfaction.

I grab my coat and take the stairs up to the door to the barn two at a time, filled with an energetic excitement. The distance between the tasting room and where I am is not large, but I'm impatient to get to Ashley. When I open the door and see her pulling on her coat, my heart swells with anticipation.

"Hey, sweet girl."

She turns to me with a smile on her face. "Hi." I close the space between us and cup her face in my hands and kiss her deeply. She meets me stroke for stroke of our tongues, and her little moans of pleasure hit me everywhere like mini lightning bolts.

"I've got a surprise for you," I murmur against her lips, feeling them curve upward in response.

"I like your surprises," she whispers, her eyes shining with happiness. I kiss the tip of her nose, her cheeks and finally her mouth again. Then I take her hands in mine, bring them to my lips, and press a kiss to her knuckles.

"Finn?" she teases, nodding her head toward the door. "My surprise?" Her eagerness is adorable, so I lead her outside, locking the tasting room behind us.

When we get to the entrance to the cellar, I open the door and the dancing light of the candles shines up the stairs, illuminating Ashley's face and the expression of wonder and anticipation I see there.

"What is all this?" she asks as she slowly descends into the cellar. I watch her face, enthralled by the play of emotions. Happiness, excitement, desire, surprise, it's exactly what I hoped for. I help her out of her coat, and hang it on a hook beside the entrance before taking my own off. Ashley watches me, and when she takes in my clothes, with my shirtsleeves rolled up and dress pants on, her tongue darts out to lick her lips. "Good grief, you're sexy."

My laugh escapes me and I hang up my coat, taking her hand to lead her over to the table that I have the wine set up on. "Thank you. Coming from the most beautiful woman I've ever met, that means a lot." I can see her blush, even in the candle-light, and I tug her forward into my arms. "I mean that, Ashley. You're stunning. Inside, outside, everywhere. Thank you for taking a chance on me, on us."

Chapter Twenty-Two

Ashley

Well, shoot. How am I meant to stay standing when he says something like that?

With his tattooed forearms on display, his hair perfectly styled, and the hella sexy, formal vibe of his outfit, Finn is pushing all my arousal buttons. Add in this incredibly sweet setup and those romantic words, and I'm putty in his arms. Settling onto the stool that he's pulled out for me, I drink in the man standing on the other side of the table. This is clearly Finn in his element. He's confident and in charge. I honestly never thought pouring wine could be sexy, but somehow it is. When he's got four glasses lined up in front of me, two white and two red, he turns the full force of his magnetism on me.

"Alright. It's time to advance your wine education." He affects an arrogant air as he says this, turning his nose up slightly and looking at me through narrowed eyes as he slides the first glass toward me. But he can't seem to hold it for long before his face relaxes into a smile. "By the time we're done here, you'll have an entirely different appreciation for, what did you call my job? Squishing grapes?"

I giggle and let my head fall forward. "I'm so sorry. That was petty of me to say." Finn's hand gently tips my chin up and my gaze follows the ink covered muscle of his arms up until it meets his gaze.

"It's fine, sweet girl. I know I needed to pull the stick out of my ass and stop being a jerk to you. I deserved your comment, and more."

I'm flustered. How do I respond to what amounts to an apology that doesn't even feel necessary? To avoid having to say anything, I lift the glass in front of me and go to take a sip, but he stops me.

"Not so fast. You need to learn how to appreciate the wine first. This first one is a Pinot Gris. I want you to sniff it first, inhale the aromas and tell me what you smell." He demonstrates, then hands the glass to me. The heat in his eyes is intense, focused, hot.

Without letting my gaze leave his, I bring the glass to my nose and breathe in deeply. "Mmm. It's flowery, but in a subtle way. Is that...citrus or something?"

He nods. "Yes, very good. Now take a small sip and let it sit on your tongue." I do as he says and an explosion of flavour hits me. I've never slowed down to truly enjoy wine this way. It's sensual, feeling the wine in so many different ways.

"It's delicious," I say, taking another sip. Finn gives me a smile of approval.

"I'm glad you like it. That is from my grandfather's vineyard in northern France."

"Is that why you love winemaking? Because of your grandfather?" Curiosity fills me as I realize I know so little about Finn's family. I know his body intimately, but not him, the man. At the hospital he told me about spending summers in France, but this feels like I'm peeling back another layer and seeing a deeper side to the man I'm falling for.

"Yes. During the summers I spent over there, we would be outside with the grapes all day." Finn's voice is rich with fondness. "He taught me how to care for the vines, and when I was old enough, he had me help with blending." He chuckles. "I was ten when he gave me my first taste. I spit it out and said he was crazy. He just smiled and said one day I would understand."

"Underage drinking? How rebellious," I tease, my hand finding his on the table. He laces our fingers together and squeezes gently before releasing me and passing the next glass over.

"Now a Viognier. This one we're making here. The grapes come from the Okanagan, and I take it from raw juice and turn it into one of my absolute favourite wines."

He seems eager to see my response to this one, so I follow his earlier instructions to slow down and savour the taste. I swirl the glass, full of golden liquid, then inhale deeply. "Oh, peaches." I glance up to see his nod of approval. I take a small sip, and the rich, heady flavour fills my mouth. I close my eyes to really savour it. "It makes me think of tropical places. Moonlight. Romance."

When my eyes flutter open, Finn is staring at me with such intensity, my lips part on a gasp. He strides around the table and spins me on my stool before leaning down and kissing me, so deeply its as if he's trying to taste the wine himself.

"God, you're so damn sexy. I can't wait."

The rumble of his words sends a shiver down my spine, and I wrap my arms around his waist, tugging him closer so he stands between my legs.

"I don't want to wait."

Finn lifts me into his arms with ease, my legs wrapping around him. After a second or two of silently gazing at each other, our passion burning hotter and hotter between us, he kisses me again, his tongue darting out to tangle with mine. We never lose contact with our lips as he turns and walks a few steps before lowering me down to the ground. How he's strong enough to do this is a question for another time because all I can think of right now is getting his clothes off so I can feel him. All of him.

My hands scramble at the buttons on his shirt. I want to take my time and unwrap him like a delicious present, but need is overtaking me and I fumble trying to get to what I want.

"Easy there, Ash," he teases, pulling back and making quick work of his shirt. When his chest is bare he lowers back down and runs his nose up the column of my neck. "Mmm. You smell better than any wine."

"Finn," I moan as he captures my earlobe in his mouth, biting down softly. He lifts the hem of my sweater and I rise up just enough for him to help me take it off. Then his hands are everywhere, running paths over my skin, tracing lines that leave nothing but heat and desire in their wake. He moves down my body, methodically undoing my jeans and sliding them down my legs. But this time it isn't his hands that move over my skin, it's his lips, pressing kisses to every inch that is bared as he removes my pants and underwear at the same time. I'm wearing only my bra, and thank God it's one of my sexier ones. Once more, Finn lets his nose lead the way as he nuzzles up my leg, alternating between warm swipes of his tongue and gentle nips of his teeth everywhere that is sensitized, which right now is essentially my entire body.

"Fuck, Ash." He sucks my inner thigh into his mouth, probably leaving a mark, but I don't care. "If I say I've waited a lifetime to have you at my mercy like this, do you believe me?" he says softly, his hands caressing my hips. I peer down my body to see him between my legs, staring at me with such reverence it takes my breath away, despite how dirty his words are.

"I wouldn't say it's been a lifetime, but it's been long enough. So why are you keeping me waiting now?" My voice is hoarse with desire and it masks the teasing nature of my response, but Finn understands. He smirks at me, then drags his thumb up and down my slit leisurely. My hips arch off the floor toward him and my head falls back with a moan that intensifies at the first swipe of his warm tongue. As he said, I am at his mercy right now. One arm is pinning me down while the other holds my folds open to his mouth. That doesn't stop me from writhing underneath him, the sounds coming from me turning more animalistic with every thrust and lick.

"Oh God, Finn, I'm so close," I whine, unable to contain myself. My hands reach up to cup my breasts, still held in place with my bra. I pinch my nipples and the rasp of the lace on my skin is almost too much combined with the feel of his thick fingers sliding in and out of me.

One hand snaps down to grab his head and hold him in place when he hits that magical spot inside of me, and he groans in response, sending shockwaves through my system. My orgasm is a kaleidoscope of colour, exploding in front of me, inside of me, and all around me.

I have no clue how much time passes with me just laying spread-eagled on the blankets, my chest heaving with every breath. Eventually I become aware of Finn lying next to me, his hand resting on my stomach. My head turns to find him looking at me with what I can only describe as a goofy grin on his face. It draws an answering smile on mine.

"Hey."

A soft laugh escapes me at his simple greeting. "Hi."

"I didn't think it was possible to be *more* attracted to you. But that...you were spectacular." Finn bends down and kisses my forehead, my nose, and finally my lips. Who is this man, so sweet and romantic? How can he be the same man who talked so dirty earlier?

"How good does your knee feel?"

His brow furrows slightly in confusion. "It's fine. Why?"

I untangle myself from his body and rise up onto my knees before turning over and facing away from him. "Because we haven't done my favourite position yet."

Finn groans, but instead of coming up behind me like I thought he would, he gently pulls me back down to the blankets.

"Sweet girl, it's fine, but it's not *kneeling on a hard floor* fine. Fuck. I'm sorry. Clearly I didn't think this plan through. Can we save that for when we've got a bed?"

He sounds so tormented, I can't even be annoyed or embarrassed. Especially not when he maneuvers me onto my side, propping my head up on one of the pillows, and lines himself up behind me.

"How about we...modify slightly?"

I open my mouth to answer, but no words come out when he snaps open my bra, slides under my neck and around to my front to fondle a breast with one hand, while the other snakes over my hip and zeroes in on my clit with exquisite precision. His lips find the back of my neck, and the combination of touch in all three zones has me forgetting all about any other position in no time.

"I promise I'll make it up to you," he murmurs against my skin.

"I'm good. Really good," I manage to say. I feel his smile, then I hear him reach over somewhere behind him, and then the telltale sound of a foil packet being opened. When he shifts back against my back, I roll my hips against him. We're a tangle of legs and arms, but somehow, I find his dick, rock hard and throbbing. I lift my top leg slightly and he shifts his hips forward to line up with my entrance. It's an entirely new experience for me, being taken from behind while lying on my side like this, and with his first thrust I quickly start to realize I might like it as much as when I'm on my hands and knees. Granted, I only discovered that position because it was the only one that brought me even close to coming with my ex.

But I'm not thinking about him right now. I'm thinking about Finn's dick sliding in and out of me, his fingers playing expertly with my clit, and his lips covering my neck and shoulders in deep, drugging kisses.

"Turn to me, babe," he commands, and I twist my upper body so our mouths can meet. His tongue thrusts in at the same time as his cock and I scream into the kiss. I'm truly at his mercy, with his leg wrapped over mine, his hand pinning me in place with its focus on my clit, and his other hand holding my breast. I've never felt so out of control, and so completely safe at the same time.

"Oh shit, Ashley," I hear him grunt when I start to clench myself around him, another orgasm barreling toward me.

"I can't wait, Finn. You're just...oh God, it's so good," I gasp. He pinches my nipple, hard, and that mix of pain and pleasure is all it takes for my body to stiffen and then release in another spectacular climax. Finn follows behind me with a roar of my name, and I feel him spill inside of me with every wild thrust until his body slows and stops. I can feel his chest rising and falling rapidly against my back, and I wonder if he can feel my heart fluttering in my chest.

We stay there for a moment, and I can only assume he's finding his way back to awareness just as I am. I can feel the hard floor beneath us now, and I'm glad Finn changed up the plan. The candles have all burned down to small flames, and it's dark enough that I can only just see the outline of the wine racks on the wall in front of me.

"The sommelier in me is offended we didn't finish the tasting," Finn comments lazily, his hand running up and down my arm. I turn onto my other side to face him and cuddle in closer.

"Is the man in you offended?" I ask slyly, earning a rumbling laugh that reverberates through me. Finn flips me onto my back and is hovering over me before I can say anything else.

"Not at all." His head comes down to kiss me slowly, leisurely. This kiss feels different from any other one. There's a depth behind it, an emotion that scares me a little. I push that thought aside and try to bring my focus back to the here and now. One of the candles Finn lit flickers out, and the intimate darkness around us grows even more pronounced.

We stay like that, kissing, exploring each other with our mouths and our hands for a while. Truthfully, I have no sense of time right now. It could be midnight for all I know. But eventually, Finn pulls back with a groan.

"Damnit woman, you're too tempting." He stands up, roots around on the floor and pulls on his pants commando.

I raise myself up on my elbows and watch him appreciatively. "Why is that a problem, exactly?"

He gives me a crooked smile. "Because. There's a lot more I want to do to you that I can't do on a hard cellar floor. Now get dressed, sweet girl."

"Fine," I huff. "But I hope that wine is coming back with us."

CHAPTER TWENTY-THREE

Finn

I wimped out. Not in terms of pleasure, hell no. I made damn sure to take care of Ashley, several times in fact.

I wimped out in terms of talking to her.

After our wine cellar date, Ashley and I went back to the Airbnb and I made good on my promise. In the comfort of a bed, we played with all the positions, and discovered that her favourite is also one of mine. At least, it certainly is when it's *her* bent over the bed and it's *her* ass I get to hold on to. We fell asleep soon after that round, but the next morning when we were lying together in a peaceful silence, I should have asked what her plans were. Hell, I should have told her I was moving back to my house this weekend.

Instead, I said nothing. Call it fear of messing up what we've got, call it fear of rejection, call it whatever you want, all I know is I feel like a fucking idiot for burying my head in the sand and not dealing with this.

But with every day that passes, I find myself starting to feel more and more anxious, mostly about our future. I have to ask her where we stand. I have to know if she's going to stay in Dogwood Cove. Because this woman could be it for me, judging by the intensity of emotion I've got toward her. But the way she talks about her dad and everything she did back in the city, the restaurants and shops she misses, makes me wonder if I'm the only one feeling that way.

Tonight we're over at Ethan and Summer's house with all of our friends for a poker night. According to Ethan, these nights used to be guys only, but Reid's girlfriend Abby is some kind of poker champ, and insisted the ladies be included, so here we are. Ethan, Jackson, Reid, Abby, and myself all seated around the table playing Texas Hold'em, with Summer, Mila, Serena, Paige, and Ashley hanging out in the living room with snacks.

Everything's going fine until we take a break between rounds and head into the other room to hang out with the girls.

"Do you need any help moving your stuff out of the Airbnb this weekend?"

Ethan's question, asked innocently enough, drops like a fucking bomb into the group. As if it were planned, all the conversations fade away and all eyes turn to me and Ashley. I peek at her out of the corner of my eye and wince when I see her gaze downcast on her hands folded in her lap.

"Ah, no thanks. I'm okay." My words land hollow in the silence. But it doesn't last long. Someone picks up on the awkwardness and starts talking about a trip to Vegas they want to take in the spring, and someone else, Serena I think, stands up to get another bottle of wine from the kitchen. I chance a look to Ashley, and reach my hand over to cover hers. "I was going to tell you, I just haven't had the chance," I say in a low enough voice that hopefully only Ashley hears. The last thing we need right now is more attention on us and my apparent fuck up.

She turns a bright smile to me, but it doesn't reach her eyes. "All good. I'm happy your house is fixed," she says in a way too chipper voice. She squeezes my fingers, then stands up abruptly. "Just going to grab something from the kitchen."

I don't let go of her hand, forcing her to stop and face me when she goes to walk away. "Ash. Are we okay?"

Another smile, slightly more genuine, but still laced with something I don't want to see. "Of course. No big deal."

She gently tugs her hand away and I let her go. Something's definitely *not* okay, and it's my fault.

"Sorry about that, man, I figured she knew." Ethan sits down next to me.

I lean back on the sofa and close my eyes briefly. "Nothing for you to apologize for. I should've mentioned it to her."

"Why didn't you?" he asks, curiosity lacing his words.

I let out a soft snort of derision. "Honestly? I have no fucking clue. Because I'm an idiot? Chickenshit? Completely useless at relationships?"

"None of that is true." Mila drops down on the couch beside me. These two have known me the longest out of anyone here, a fact that I'm grateful for right now. Maybe they can shed some light on what the hell is wrong with me.

"Yeah, you definitely made an idiot move, but you're not chickenshit and you're not useless at relationships," Ethan adds. "Have you two talked about her plans yet?"

Mila leans forward to stare at her brother. "Of course he has." She turns to poke me in the side. "You have, right?"

I shake my head.

"Okay, maybe you are useless. Finn McNeil, you have to talk to that girl, and soon. Before she goes back to Vancouver thinking you aren't in love with her."

My heart stutters at Mila's words. In love? Me? The very thought of that being true makes my anxiety spike. How can I be in love with a woman who has yet to even call me her boyfriend? A woman who, as far as I know, plans on leaving in a few weeks, if not sooner, to go back to her life in Vancouver. What would that even be like for us? It's not as if I can pack up and move with her, not now that the winery is so close to opening. But can I really ask her to upend her life and move here for me?

"I just wish I knew what she was thinking."

Mila thumps me on the shoulder. "Then ask her, you dummy."

My hand comes up to rub where she hit me. "No shit. I know I need to ask her, but it would help if I had even a slight idea what she might say." My head snaps around to look at her as the obvious answer occurs to me. "Wait. Mila. You guys talk, has she said anything to you?"

Mila raises both of her hands up in the air. "Hell no. Chicks before dicks, my friend."

I close my eyes against the groan of frustration and uncertainty that bubbles up inside. "Great. That's helpful."

"Ethan, Finn, we're gonna get started again, you coming?" Reid calls to us from the table.

Ethan stands up with a friendly cuff to my shoulder and heads to join them, leaving just Mila and I on the couch. At that moment, Ashley comes back in the room and glances over at us before joining Paige by the fireplace.

"Don't let her go, Finn." Mila's not normally the serious one of our group, so her somber tone hits differently.

"I don't want to," I reply honestly.

"Then put away your insecurities and talk to her."

If only it were that simple.

By this point I think Ashley and I are the masters of awkward silences. It seems to be a running theme between us, and it's one I'm really getting sick of. How can two people have such amazing chemistry and connection most of the time, but as soon as something gets in between us, we revert to virtual strangers?

At the Airbnb, Ashley gives me a smile when I open her door and help her out of my car. She laces her fingers with mine and even leans her head on my shoulder, giving me some hope that maybe she's just processing everything. Once we're inside, we go through the motions of getting ready for bed. We still haven't spoken, but it feels slightly more normal now, less tense.

When we're settled in bed, I open my arms and beckon Ashley over. Thank God she snuggles right in, resting her cheek on my bare chest. I'd love nothing more than to strip her naked, bury myself in her, and ignore the last hour or so of tension, but I know I can't neglect things any longer.

"I really am sorry I didn't tell you about my house sooner." I press a kiss to the top of her head. She likes that I've found that gesture always makes her nuzzle in closer. Tonight is no different, as she turns to kiss my chest in return.

"It's fine, Finn, really. It's not normal for couples to live together right from the beginning."

Part of me wants to latch onto the fact that she called us as couple, but I can't entirely rely on that one word for the answers I need. Besides, she might be saying the right words to try and reassure me, but there's something missing in her voice. Something that makes me doubt what she says is truly how she feels.

"We can have quite a bit of fun with the big shower at my place, and I can cook us dinner."

"Mmhmm." Ashley yawns delicately. "Hey, I'm really tired. Do you mind if we talk more tomorrow?"

My stomach drops.

"Yeah, of course. Goodnight, sweet girl." I tip her chin up to kiss her lips and press her mouth with a desperation I'm not used to feeling. Her hand comes up to caress my cheek, and the familiar expression of dazed pleasure I'm so used to seeing on her beautiful face when we kiss is there, reassuring me slightly.

But it's not enough to stop me from lying awake long after Ashley's breathing settles into the slow pattern of sleep, worrying that I'm about to lose the best thing that ever happened to me.

CHAPTER TWENTY-FOUR

Ashley

Finn moved back to his house five days ago, and I'm still not used to having the Airbnb to myself. Even though we've spent almost every night together at his place, I still come back here to shower and get dressed each morning before heading to the winery.

It's weird.

It's weird that he didn't tell me his house was ready, it's weird that he just packed up and moved out Sunday morning while I was meeting the girls for breakfast at The Nutty Muffin, and it's weird that he hasn't asked me to stay with him.

Okay, maybe that last one *shouldn't* be weird since we've only been seeing each other for a few weeks, and we haven't even had a conversation about where our relationship is going long-term, or what our relationship even is, but still...it feels weird. There's a nasty voice in my head that keeps whispering to me that I was a convenient body when Finn was at the Airbnb, but that the little bubble of domestic bliss we had there couldn't possibly translate to the real world, given how little we actually know each other. But my heart doesn't want to listen to that voice. My heart misses having him down the hall, hearing him get ready in the morning, and driving to work together.

Trusting Finn, trusting what we have, and its capacity to be something real is hard. I could easily blame my ex for cheating on me and destroying my trust in men, but that's not it. I do believe that Finn wouldn't hurt me intentionally, and I do trust that our chemistry and attraction is mutual. Where things get less black and white is when I remember how he treated me when we first met. Can his feelings really change so dramatically in such a short time? He was a jerk to me in the beginning. No, he was an asshole to me. So anytime I think about talking to him about our future, I freeze. Because when something seems too good to be true, it often is. Just look at any fad diet, reality TV show, or wrinkle cream commercial.

Apparently, the cynical side of me that I thought was fading away, courtesy of Dogwood Cove's unique charm, is back in full force.

FINN: Hey sweet girl, just checking you're still coming over later tonight?

Despite my misgivings, seeing his name pop up on my phone brings a smile to my face. I put down my hair brush and pick up my phone to type out an answer.

ASHLEY: Yup. Should I pick up some box wine from the store?

FINN: BLASPHEMY! How dare you utter those words in my presence

ASHLEY: LOL okay, so Barefoot Moscato it is.

I laugh out loud as I type. This, the easy banter between us, this is why I'm so conflicted. I've never felt such a connection with someone, even if it is accompanied by more uncertainty and doubt than I've ever had as well.

FINN: ...

FINN: ...

FINN: I'm changing the locks on my door.

I know he's teasing, but I can't hold back a wince. Nor do I hold back in my response.

ASHLEY: That doesn't mean much since I don't have a key.

I start to chew on my nail, waiting to see his response. Shit. Maybe I should unsend that? No, it's too late, I'm sure he's seen it. Oh God, that made me sound like a needy brat. Shit, shit, shit, shit.

FINN: Good point. We should change that.

My phone clatters down to the bathroom counter in front of me and my head falls forward, letting a curtain of my hair fall around me. For a long minute I just breathe. This infuriating, adorably sweet, completely confusing, sexy man. Doesn't he know how that kind of message makes me feel? Can't he tell how crazy he's making me? You can't imply that you're going to give a woman a key when you haven't even had the whole boyfriend/girlfriend conversation, you just can't.

I realize at this point, there's a high likelihood we're both dancing around the subject, avoiding it like the proverbial hot potato. It is starting to feel as immature and stupid as it sounds. But after what I went through the last time I opened my heart to a man, I'm hesitant to be the one to put it all on the line.

I just can't do it.

ASHLEY: See you after book club.

This is the second book club meeting I've gone to, and I've realized that it's less about the books and more about the friendships between these women. Case in point, tonight Mila brought pastries, including one very phallic shaped, cream filled eclair. When the cream filling jokes started, we were all dying with laughter, trying to explain it to Paige who just couldn't see what we could. I don't think she's a virgin, and based on the conversation points and discussion questions she creates for each book, she's not exactly innocent. But sometimes the subtext seems to just elude her. It reminds me of when Sarah and I were in school and how naïve and innocent we were back then. Our private school's version of sex ed raised so many questions, and we spent many nights giggling together, secretly reading her mom's Harlequin romance books. Basically, the situation makes me miss Sarah fiercely, and I vow to call her tomorrow. I wish she was here and could meet everyone.

Eventually we talk about the book, a royalty romance that I found way over-the-top, but highly entertaining. And then, over our third glass of wine, the conversation veers away from the book. But I've been lulled into a false sense of security by the fact that no one has mentioned Finn, or what's going on with us. Which is why Serena's next words have me choking on my wine until my eyes water.

"Has Finn asked you to move in with him yet?"

When I catch my breath and swipe away the tears, I shake my head. "Ah, no. He has not."

Serena tilts her head to the side. "Hmm, is that trouble in paradise I'm sensing? You know, we're practically experts at relationships in crisis by now. Not only did we read about them in book club last year, but look around you." She gestures to the other women. "Three out of the five of us are happily in love, but only because *we* played a part in fixing whatever went wrong. Because men are idiots, so something always goes wrong. Basically, we're relationship gurus. So spill."

Summer starts to clap when Serena finishes and Mila and Abby quickly join in. I notice Paige doesn't, but she seems to be the more serious one of the group, so I guess it doesn't surprise me.

"I couldn't have said it better myself, girl," Mila cheers, lifting her glass of wine and tipping it to Serena.

"Serena's right," Summer says, softly placing her hand on my thigh. "Several of us have been through tough times with our guys, but we've come out the other side of it happier than ever. Let us help?"

"There's really nothing to help with," I say nervously. "We just aren't at that point, you know? It was fun when we were at the Airbnb together, but that wasn't real. Real life, I mean. That was just some weird little bubble we were in for a while."

"A bubble where you had a hot, live-in boyfriend, with dick any time you wanted it," Serena states matter-of-factly.

"He's not my boyfriend," I'm quick to respond, then take a gulp of my drink, feeling it burn with the acid my words are churning up.

"Really? Because it seemed like..." Summer starts to talk, then trails off. "I don't know. I guess it just seemed like you guys were really close."

"I mean, we are," I stammer out. "But it's just not...I don't know. We haven't talked about it."

"You've been too busy having sex."

My head whips up. There's no judgment in Mila's tone, but the words land like an accusation.

"I...we..."

"Hey, it's all good. Finn's hot, I don't blame you. But he's also got a heart of gold. And a lot of love to give. That's all I'm saying."

It's not the first time Mila has said something like this to me. But it is the first time that the word *love* hits me. I give her a small smile and nod of understanding. Then, thankfully, the conversation shifts onto Abby's daughter Layla, and the horseback riding lessons she's starting out at Crescent Ranch, located close to Westport, the nearest big city.

"I'm telling you, it's a good thing he isn't the instructor, or Reid would never let me take her there for lessons," Abby giggles. She's telling us all about one of the ranch hands who is apparently drop dead gorgeous. "What is it about a man in Wranglers and cowboy boots? Ooh boy."

The girls all laugh and I join in half-heartedly. But in reality, my head is not here with my friends. My head and my heart are somewhere else with a very specific winemaker in mind.

When I get to Finn's house that evening, I let myself in. He normally leaves the front door unlocked when he knows I'm coming over late. I drop my purse and coat in the front entryway, lock the door, and make my way to the bedroom. What I find there is so heart achingly sweet, I'm pretty sure my ovaries combust. Finn is fast asleep on his bed, curled over on his side with one arm stretched out. On the pillow where I would sleep, there's a single red rose. The only light comes from a scattering of battery-operated candles throughout the room, reminding me of our night in the wine cellar. The horny side of me wants to wake him up and enjoy the romantic evening he planned out, but I also know that for him to fall asleep so early must mean he's exhausted. The long days getting the winery up and running are catching up to him. So instead, I quietly get ready for bed in the bathroom, then after placing the rose on the bedside table, I crawl into bed beside him and let sleep overtake me.

The next morning I'm woken up by Finn's magical tongue circling my belly button and his strong hands gripping my hips.

"Wha? Finn?" I say sleepily, and those seem to be the magical words. He wastes no time, yanking my shorts down and diving into me, licking and sucking with such intensity it feels like no time at all before I'm screaming out his name as my hips arch off the bed. I'm only vaguely aware of him tugging my shorts back into place and kissing his way back up my body until he's stretched out beside me.

"Now we can go to work," he says, ridiculously satisfied with himself. I swat at him as I giggle and drop my other arm over my eyes.

"Nope, can't work. You broke me."

Suddenly I feel his lips on mine. "Come on, sweet girl. Let's get our work over with so I can have a redo on last night."

My arms fall to his back and start to stroke lazily up and down. "And what exactly was last night meant to be?"

Oh Lord, the nervous blush peeking through his stubble is just too much. I run my fingers through my hair, ignoring the pang in my heart. It's too much to let myself believe that last night he was going to tell me we should be together, like boyfriend and girlfriend, falling in love together. But the hope is there.

"Last night was meant to be me taking care of my girl." He drops a kiss to my forehead. But before I can respond, he lifts himself off of me and strolls toward the bathroom. "Now hurry up. Can't be late for work."

"I'm freelance. I set my own schedule," I call out to him teasingly. I hear the shower turn on and then his head pops around the door.

"Yeah, well, I hired you. And I say we need to get to work." He winks, then disappears again. I fall back into the bed with a small laugh, shaking my head.

"Let's go, sweet girl! Get up!"

With one final roll of my eyes that I know he can't see, but it feels good all the same, I drag myself out of bed and go to the bathroom. Opening the door to the shower, I step in, arch my eyebrow at the cocky grin he gives me as he lathers his head with shampoo, then I drop to my knees.

"Still think we need to get to work on time?" I ask primly as his hand comes down and tangles in my hair.

"Fuuuck," he groans as I take his semihard cock in my hand and begin to stroke it gently. "We can be late."

I wrap my lips around his tip and hum before sucking him as deep as I can go. The hot water cascades down over me, making things slippery and sensual. His moans of pleasure echo around the glass shower enclosure as I work him up and down, alternating deep sucks with long, slow licks. My tongue swirls around his tip and I bring one hand up to fondle his balls. I never put much thought toward a man's balls until now, but the way it drives Finn crazy when I do gives me a new appreciation for them.

"God. Ash." His hand tightens in my hair and his hips start to move, slowly but surely. I take the cue and increase my speed, bringing him up and over the edge into an orgasm that has him shouting out my name, his pleasure making me heavy with my own desire.

Eventually we do manage to actually shower, both of us smiling and laughing as we dry off and go to the bedroom to get dressed.

We still haven't talked about us, or our future, but this right here, this domestic, easy, comfortable togetherness is everything I've always wanted with a partner. My heart feels light and happy, and I'm starting to think that maybe Finn is telling me how he feels, just not with words.

As I'm buttoning up my blouse, my phone rings and my eyes dart down to the beside table where it sits out of habit. Wait. Why the fuck is my dad's housekeeper calling me? I grab it and answer quickly.

"Mrs. Crenshaw? Is everything okay?"

Chapter Twenty-Five

Finn

Five days, and only three text messages. That's the sum total of the communication I've had with Ashley since she ran out of my house.

The phone call from some woman, who apparently works for her dad, made all the colour drain from her face. I tried to hug her, to offer comfort, but she pushed me away and frantically finished dressing, grabbed her purse, and left. The only details I got out of her was that her dad was sick, and she had to go.

When she eventually got in touch with me later that evening she told me her father was admitted to hospital with a suspected heart attack. That was text message number one. When I immediately responded that I would come over to help her any way I could, message number two told me not to come, and that she hopes to be back on the island to finish the tasting room soon.

Finish the tasting room. Not see me.

The third message was a weird one. It simply said *I'm sorry.* Sorry for what? I have no idea because she hasn't answered my text asking that exact question. It fucking kills me to think she's over there with her only surviving parent sick and in the hospital, and she thinks she has to apologize to me. But the last thing I want to do is cause her more stress, or bother her if she really doesn't want me around.

Except I miss her.

I miss her when I'm out running and I go past the Airbnb. I miss her when I'm at the winery trying to work and I walk into the tasting room. I miss her when I go to The Nutty Muffin and only buy one scone, not two.

I'm turning into a grumpy sap from missing her.

Which is why I let the guys drag me out to Hastings tonight, where I've been sitting at the bar, moping over a bottle of beer Dean pushed my way when I walked in.

"Her dad has a housekeeper. Aren't rich people the only ones with housekeepers?" I ask, taking a swig from my bottle of beer.

"Why the fuck does it matter?" Reid asks and I glare at him.

"It doesn't. I'm just saying we're different. What if she's back in the city and decides she would rather have some city slicker guy instead of the guy who squishes grapes for a job." God, even the memory of the first time she described my work that way makes my stomach hurt.

"I'm not even going to touch the squishing grapes comment because *what the fuck*. But do you hear yourself right now? You're being an idiot. Ashley isn't like that and you know it. Besides, even if she does come from money, who the hell cares?

She doesn't act like a spoiled rich kid, so whatever. Stop whining and looking for problems that don't even exist."

Even in my current state of emotional turmoil, I know Ethan's right. Besides, this isn't me. I don't lack self-confidence, I've never once felt like my choice of vocation makes me any less than anyone else, and I certainly don't give two shits whether someone has money or not. This is me lashing out for no good reason.

"You're nervous. She left before you guys could talk about things." Dean leans back on the counter behind him, taking a sip from a bottle of water. I stare at him, with his wedding band staring me in the face. Easy for him to say I'm nervous, he's got an amazing woman who loves him and is currently carrying his child.

"Bartender's right, my friend." Reid tips his bottle of beer toward Dean, who nods his head in acknowledgment, then heads down to the other end of the bar to help another customer.

"Okay. Fine. Let's say you jackasses are right, and I am just nervous. What the hell do I do?"

"Easy. You go and get your girl." Ethan, Jackson and Reid all clink their bottles together.

Fuck.

The next morning I drive out to the winery, still consumed with questions and worries about Ashley. She's never far from my mind, and when my text this morning went unanswered, again, I banged my head against the wall in frustration. When Pierre finds me in the blending lab, I've just poured my third attempt at creating a Meritage down the drain. Finding that balance of flavour that each custom blend of red wine is famous for is not easy, and I cannot seem to get it right today.

"And what did that juice do to offend you?" Pierre asks in a far too cheerful voice. I grunt in response as I go to the sink to clean out the vials and beakers I was using for blending. "Or perhaps it is not the juice that has you upset, but rather the absence of our lovely Ashley."

I set the glass vials down carefully, then place my hands on the counter and let my head drop down to my chest.

"Do you need anything, Pierre?" I know I'm being rude, but I don't feel like making small talk. Especially not about Ashley.

"Just to know why you are not on a ferry headed toward Vancouver to be with her, and to make sure she comes back, of course."

I turn around slowly and fold my arms over my chest. "What if she doesn't want to come back?"

The look he gives me clearly says he thinks I'm an idiot. Seems to be a common theme amongst my friends these days.

"My dear Finn. You are a brilliant winemaker and a good man. But right now, you are also a fool. Go to her."

He turns on his heel and walks to the door of the lab before pausing and speaking over his shoulder to me. "She wants to come back, I am confident of it. But a woman also needs to feel wanted. And that is what I think is missing."

Goddamnit, he's right. They're all right. My hesitation is the only thing to blame for Ashley shutting me out right now. Well, that and her dad being hospitalized, I guess. She doesn't know she can want me or need me because I haven't made it clear that I'm here for her, no matter what.

I grab my phone and coat, and stride out of the blending lab, shutting off lights and locking the door behind me. I stick my head into the tasting room and find Pierre sitting calmly at a table, poring over some paperwork.

"I'll be away for the next few days."

He lifts his head to me and nods. "Good."

Two hours later, I'm on the ferry headed to the mainland, staring at my phone and trying to decide how to tell Ashley that I'm coming. I go back and forth on this for who knows how long, alternating between looking at my phone and looking out at the grey sea of the Strait of Georgia. The ferry is bringing me closer to Ashley, but I'm no closer to knowing what I'm going to say to her or how I'm going to convince her to give us a real chance.

The one thing I do decide on is not tell her I'm coming. Pierre texted me earlier with the address of her dad's house in some fancy neighbourhood in West Vancouver. My phone gives me the address for a florist in Dundarave that I plan on stopping at before finding Ashley.

Sitting in my car, waiting to disembark from the ferry, realizing I'll see Ashley very soon and finally, *finally* tell her how I feel, sends a wave of calm over me like I've never felt before. All the worry and uncertainty suddenly disappear, and with a startling clarity, I can see that all I need to do is be honest. Tell her I'm falling in love with her, tell her I want her in Dogwood Cove, and in my life.

My fingers drum on the steering wheel in time to the music playing on the radio. It's some sappy love song, which I guess is fitting. I don't even absorb the luxurious homes I drive past on my way into town, my focus is lasered in on Ashley and nothing else.

Fate is smiling on me when I find a parking spot right outside the florist shop. I park and head inside, and walk out twenty minutes later with a bouquet of bright yellow and pink flowers. The colours are vibrant, and even though they shouldn't work together, they do. Kind of like me and Ashley.

I'm about to climb into my car when I see a familiar car. The same car that was parked outside of my house just a few days ago.

Ashley.

My gaze darts everywhere trying to find her. But when I do find her, she's not alone. The woman I'm falling for, the woman I've been obsessing about for days is sitting at a small table inside a restaurant across from a man who's definitely not her father. She's smiling, and as I stand there, completely frozen, she tips her head back and laughs.

That's my laugh. That's my smile. That's my hand she's reaching out to cover his with.

I know my possessive reaction is a defense mechanism, just as I know I should go inside and talk to her. After all, this could be nothing. It could be an old client or a former colleague. But just as I'm working up to doing that, she stands from the table and this other man pulls her into his arms.

They're hugging.

But Ashley doesn't hug.

Fuck, she's resting her cheek on his chest, and even though she's turned away from me, her comfort around this guy is evident, even from a distance. I take a step to the door, then I freeze in horror. The flowers I'm clutching fall to the ground as I watch the other man bend down and kiss the top of her head, giving *my woman* physical affection so freely when I know just how hard it is to get her to accept it.

I pivot on my heel and walk back to my car swiftly. With little attention to the road and other drivers, I pull out into traffic and drive back the way I came, all the way to the ferry terminal and all the way onto the next boat headed to the island.

It's only once we're underway and the distance is growing between me and what I just witnessed that I let my hands uncurl from the tense grip on my steering wheel, and let the reality of everything sink in.

At least now I know why she's sorry.

Chapter Twenty-Six

Ashley

It's surprising to me, how strange it feels to be back on the mainland after just over a month in Dogwood Cove. It's funny how quickly you can adjust, I guess.

When I first got off the ferry, I drove straight to Vancouver General Hospital to see my dad. He'd suffered a mild heart attack and was admitted to the cardiac floor. The first few days I don't think I slept much, and I only went back to Dad's house to shower and change my clothes in between days at the hospital by his bedside. He underwent an angiogram and stenting to clear the blockage. Those hours sitting in an uncomfortable chair, waiting for the doctor to come and talk to me were pure torture. I don't remember my mom being sick, I was too young when she died of cancer. But being in that hospital, worrying that my only remaining parent might die was by far the hardest thing I've ever gone through.

My phone was filling with messages from Finn and everyone else back in Dogwood Cove, and eventually I started leaving it in my car. I just couldn't handle all the concern and questions. Especially because no matter how much I miss them, especially Finn, my mind has taken to catastrophizing everything. What if it hadn't been a mild heart attack? What if it was something more serious and I couldn't get home in time? What if my father died and I wasn't here...

Yeah, needless to say my head hasn't been a very pleasant place to be lately. I know I need to reach out, especially to Finn. It's not right for me to freeze him out like this, but I don't even know what to say. When he offered to come here right after I left, I wanted so badly to say yes. But at the same time, what would that mean? Him being here, meeting my dad, are we really at that point? I want to say we are, but our stupid lack of communication means I can't be sure. God, I was such an idiot for not talking to him.

Thankfully Dad was able to come home after just a few days in hospital, but he needs quite a bit of help. Mrs. Crenshaw has been amazing with meals and groceries, and her husband, who has always done general maintenance and yard upkeep ever since I was a child, helped me move my Dad's bed down to his office so he doesn't have to do the stairs.

Dad and I have spent hours this week just talking about anything and everything, except, that is, Finn and my time on the island. Aside from telling him I enjoyed the work and the town, I've stayed far away from that topic. Not because I don't want to talk to him, but because I just don't know what to say. How do you explain to your father that you fell hard for a man you've only known a few weeks? For that matter, how do I tell my only parent that I want to move away?

Dad has always been the pragmatic one, the logical thinker. When I've faced any problems, he's the parent who would sit me down and have me make a pro-con list. The difference is, this time, the only con to moving to Dogwood Cove and being with Finn is leaving my father behind.

"Sweet pea, if you frown any harder, your face will stay like that."

His voice still sounds frail, but it's getting stronger by the day. I soften my expression and turn to see Dad shuffling into the kitchen. He's a shadow of the strong man he normally is, but I'm filled with so much gratitude that he's still here to tease me.

"Dad, what are you doing out of bed?" I chastise him gently as he makes his way to a stool that lines the counter.

"They said no heavy lifting or driving, not *no moving*," he retorts. I take a deep breath. His heart attack scared us both, but he certainly seems to be handling it better than I am.

"I just made some peppermint tea, want some?"

He nods and I busy myself with pouring a second cup. I pass it over to him and go to sit beside him, carefully letting my head fall to his shoulder.

"What's going on in that beautiful head of yours, honey?"

I lift my head and give him a small smile before taking a sip of tea. I'm not really sure how to answer his question.

"A lot, Dad. A lot."

He wraps his arm around my shoulder and squeezes gently. "Talk to me, sweet pea."

"I think I fell in love."

To his credit, my dad doesn't laugh at my blurted confession. In fact, he seems to be taking the news way more calmly than I am. It's the first time I've let myself really admit just how deep my feelings for Finn really go. Those six words open a floodgate inside of me, and suddenly I'm tripping over myself, trying to tell Dad everything.

"His name is Finn and he's the vintner at Pierre's winery. Well, he co-owns it, I guess. And he was so grumpy when I first got there, but eventually we worked it out. He's got such a good heart, and when we're together I just know that he's really there with me. He's not distracted or thinking about something else, he's with me. And even though he drives me crazy sometimes, and he confuses me almost all the time, he also feels right, you know?"

Dad's slow chuckle fills my ear. "Oh, my darling daughter, I do know. That's how it was for your mother and I. We were at odds for years before I finally convinced her to give me a chance."

I sit up straight and face him. "I've never heard that story. What do you mean at odds?"

"Come, let's go to the living room so I can be comfortable." Dad stands up slowly and we make our way to the cozy, lived-in leather couches that have been here since I was a teenager. I help Dad get settled, then take the navy blue blanket I gave him for part of his Christmas gift years ago, and sit down at the other end before draping it over my feet.

"Your mother and I met in university, you remember?" Dad looks at me with an eyebrow raised. At my nod, he continues. "She was smart. So damn smart. And she just loved to be the best in class. Too bad for her, so did I." He chuckles, shaking his head ruefully. I take a sip of my tea and wait. Hearing stories about my mom is something I never get tired of.

"Our program was small, only about twenty of us in the entire cohort. And your mother was one of only three women. There just wasn't the same representation of women in business back then. She was a firecracker, though, and never let any of us treat her as less deserving of a spot than we were simply by being men." Dad pauses and I can tell from the expression on his face he's lost in the memories. "She and I battled for top marks all year long. And outside of class was no better. It seemed we would run across each other everywhere, whether it was our volunteer positions in the student union, or the lineup at the cafeteria. Every time she would see me, she'd roll her eyes, march up to me and say, 'imitation is the greatest form of flattery, Simon, but this is getting ridiculous.' Little did she know, it wasn't about me imitating her, it was about me desperately wanting more time with her. I was infatuated, but had no clue what to do about it. She was so strong and independent, so fierce, I didn't think I had a chance. But then, in our senior year, we had to partner up for our final project. Luck was on my side when Marian drew my name out of the hat. Forced to spend time working together gave us a new appreciation for each other, and the day we presented to the class was also the day I kissed her for the first time."

I watch Dad lift his mug of tea to his mouth and take a small sip before lowering it back down to his lap. When he turns his gaze up to me, his eyes are brimming with unshed tears and love.

"She was the love of my life, but not a day went by that she didn't make me crazy in some way. I think that spark, that energy is what kept us going. We challenged each other constantly. It was never easy, but it was always worth it."

The way he describes it makes me miss Finn fiercely. I hate that I left before he and I had a chance to talk. I want to tell him I'm falling in love with him, that I want to be with him if he'll have me.

I want to move to Dogwood Cove.

"Dad, how would you feel if I lived on the island?"

"Well, honey, I'd say it's about time."

Right away, I start to set things in motion. After talking with Dad and his doctor, as well as Mrs. Crenshaw, we worked out a plan for someone to check in on him daily. His doctor said that wasn't even necessary given how well he's doing, but for my peace of mind it is. I even made a reservation for the ferry tomorrow night to bring me back to Dogwood Cove one week after I left.

Last night, I spent over an hour on the phone with Sarah talking about everything. She's still my number one sounding board and I wish like hell she would come home to BC. She convinced me not to tell anyone I'm coming back. Something about it being a grand gesture, romantic surprise type thing. I'm nervous about that idea, but at the same time I know I've got some serious explaining to do, especially to Finn. I can only hope he's willing to forgive me for disappearing for a week. When I read back through our sparse text messages, I cringed. In my attempt to keep him at arm's length, I ended up being a real bitch. My dad also reamed me out when I admitted that Finn offered to be with me while he was in hospital, saying I was "a fool not to let that man love you." The truth is, it feels like too much to ask for Finn to love me back at this point. We let things get so uncertain, so confusing, I can't see how he would possibly want to give it a real try between us.

But the other thing Sarah convinced me of was this — I'm not moving to Dogwood Cove for Finn. I'm moving there for me. My happiness, my future, it lies on the island. Whether Finn is a part of that or not.

Which is why the next call I made was to Tom Coffman. As luck would have it, he was on the mainland with his husband for an interview in their adoption process. We agreed to meet for lunch today and hammered out the details of our partnership.

Starting as soon as I'm finished with the tasting room, I'll be a managing partner at Coffman Interiors. That was a big enough deal that when Tom went to hug me, I let him do it. Of course, he followed it up with a swat to my arm and firm instructions to "get my man," but that's not the point. The point is, for the first time in many months, I've got a plan, a purpose. I know what I want, and I'm damn well going to do whatever it takes to get it.

And what I want is Finn.

Chapter Twenty-Seven

I'm just pulling up to my house when my phone rings. It's my mom, and while the last thing I want to do right now is talk to someone, I know her. If I don't answer, she'll call back. Especially since I've been too wrapped up in my personal life drama to call her recently. It's times like this that I wish I wasn't so damn close with my parents.

"Hey, Mom."

"Finn? Mon cher, I can hear the sadness in your voice from here. What is wrong?"

Yep, definitely wishing my mom didn't know me quite so well right now. "I'm fine, really. Just dealing with some stuff." Maybe, just this once, she'll let it go.

Yeah right.

"Finnley Matisse McNeil." Oh shit, she pulled out my full name. "I have known you for all thirty-six years of your life. I have witnessed many moods, and many feelings. Which means when I say I can hear sadness, I know what I can hear. Talk to your maman."

I shut off the engine of my car and lean back against the seat. "Remember the designer from the winery?"

"Yes, Ashley was her name, non?"

I must take too long to confirm that because my mom hits the nail on the head, first try.

"You became close, and now you are not?"

"Something like that," I say evasively. I may be close to my mom, but the last thing I want to do is tell her how heartbroken I am. Even I have my limits.

"Well, even though you are not telling me everything..." She pauses, and I chuckle. Damn, she's good. "I sense that she is important to you if she has you this upset. So, can you fix what went wrong?"

"No. Because I didn't *do* anything wrong." My hands come up to my head, and I pull off my baseball cap. Damn thing makes me think of her anyway, and how her eyes would glow when she'd see me wearing it backwards.

"Mon cher. I adore you, you know this. But you are not without faults. Please remember that there are always two sides to everything. Have an open heart and an open mind. Is that not what your father and I have always taught you."

"I know, Mom. I know."

"Okay. I will let you go, I can tell you do not want to talk to your mother right now. Je t'aime, Finn. You are a good man. Trust your heart."

I let out a long sigh, letting her love soothe at least a part of my pain. "Thanks, Mom. I love you, too."

I hang up and go inside my house. It's just as empty feeling as it was this morning before I left. Back when I just thought Ashley was avoiding me because she was busy with her dad. Man, I would give anything to go back to that, instead of this painful new awareness I have.

It's late afternoon, still light enough out, so I change into some running clothes and lace up my shoes. I need to get rid of this energy coursing through me. Setting my music to play something that will force me into a punishing pace, I take off, making my way to some of the back roads of Dogwood Cove that weave through fields and some of the small farms. Of course, the road I'm on also goes past the Airbnb that Ashley and I stayed in. I keep my head down and sprint past.

While I run, as much as I want to ignore the voice in my head, I can't. My mom's question keeps running on repeat. Can I fix what went wrong...my immediate reaction is the same as what I said to Mom. No, of course I can't, because I didn't do anything. I'm not the one having lunch with another woman.

But then I let myself think, really think, about what Mom said next. There are always two sides. Did I have a role to play? I was an idiot for not talking to Ashley about how I felt, and for not asking her about her plans. Is that what drove her to ignore me, and literally into the arms of another man?

There's a small part of me that refuses to believe that what I saw is what I'm making it out to be. That isn't the woman I fell in love with. If I hadn't seen it myself, if someone else was trying to tell me they saw Ashley with another man, I would probably laugh at them, and tell them it was nothing. So why can't I believe that now?

Why did I turn and run, instead of facing her and asking her to explain?

It was that fucking hug.

She told me she doesn't hug people unless it's a super important occasion or someone really important to her. Hearing that felt so damn good. To know I was different, special. She liked being affectionate with me.

Which is why witnessing her so easily hugging another man was a lethal shot to my heart. I slow to a jog and then stop, panting for breath, and drop my hands to the tops of my knees. Fuck, I'm messed up. Completely destroyed. And my mom is right. I am just as much to blame as Ashley because I never talked to her.

About anything.

I let my stress and fear over my job, Pierre's reaction, and what happened back in Napa get the better of me, and I fucking screwed up. I should have told her I wanted her in my life, wanted her as my girlfriend, wanted a life with her.

It's a little ironic how I was so scared of losing Ashley that I never saw the truth. I didn't have her to begin with.

After my run, I went home, showered, and opened a bottle of La Lune Rouge Merlot, polishing off the entire bottle. At least when I decide to drink away my sorrow, I do it with something good.

This morning I'm hurting, but not too badly. I've got a healthy tolerance for wine, an occupational hazard. I dress for work without caring about my appearance. I'm spending the day in the blending lab, still trying to perfect that damn Meritage. Hoodie, jeans, baseball cap. Done.

Against my better judgment, I swing into The Nutty Muffin for breakfast, and finally, I catch a break. Mila doesn't see me, so I manage to get in and out, coffee and pastry in hand, with nothing more than some small talk with Sebastian, who's manning the cash register.

At the winery, I steer clear of the tasting room. Pierre's car isn't here yet, but I know he's due in today. I don't have any desire to face him and explain how everything went to shit yesterday. I head straight to the barn, and march down the long space to the back where my blending lab is, and dive headfirst into work, not stopping for several hours until my phone rings. When I see it's Mila, I debate ignoring her, but there's no point. Everyone is going to find out eventually, might as well be now.

"Hi," I say gruffly.

"Finn? Sorry I missed you at the bakery this morning, I didn't know you stopped by. Hey, Seb said you were heading to the winery, are you still there?" She sounds way too bubbly for me.

"Yeah, where else would I be?" I bark out.

"Geez, now I see why Ashley said you were scowly," she teases and I wince at hearing her name.

"What do you need?

"Seriously? What's wrong, Finn?" Mila's tone sobers.

"Nothing."

"Okay, if you're not gonna tell me, I'll guess. Did you spill some wine?"

"No. Mila, I don't have time for your teasing."

"Then tell me what's wrong."

"Ashley fucking screwed me over, that's what," I roar into the phone, completely fed up with everyone nosing into my business and not just letting me stew in my feelings.

"What the hell are you talking about?" Mila sounds outraged at me. What a joke. She's mad at me for telling her that Ashley broke my heart. Some friend.

I let out a harsh laugh. "I went to the mainland to be with her. And I found her hugging another guy, Mila. She doesn't hug people. And she was hugging him."

"Oh my God, Finn, it was a freaking hug. Maybe he's her cousin or something! I can't believe you're making such a big deal out of a goddamn hug. Besides, if she was with some other guy, why the hell is she *here* in Dogwood Cove, looking for you? She just called me, asking if I knew where you were. She's on her way."

"Fuck, Mila, you don't understand." I know I shouldn't take this out on Mila, but then again, she called me. She started this.

"No, you're right. I don't," Mila shrieks into the phone. "I thought you two were close. But clearly you're not. Clearly you don't know her at all if you think she could two-time you like that. Just talk to her, you idiot. Don't make me regret telling her where to find you." Mila ends the call and I resist the urge to chuck my phone against the wall. She doesn't know what she's talking about.

But wait, Ashley's here. She's in Dogwood Cove, coming to see me. A tiny flare of hope stirs inside me, but is quickly doused by reality. I can't let myself be fooled.

A short time later, I hear her car pull up outside and I take a deep breath. As much as I'm dreading this conversation, I know it has to happen. I deserve the closure. I wipe my hands and slowly walk to the front door of the barn. When I get outside, I see her sitting in her car. Our eyes meet. I cross my arms in front of my chest and wait.

When she gets out, it physically pains me to see her again. God, she's so beautiful, and she's smiling. At least, she is at first. I see the moment she takes in my defensive posture, and that smile falls from her face, morphing into one of confusion and concern.

"Finn?" She approaches me cautiously, as if I were a wild animal. I feel like one right now, caged and desperate for escape. "I'm sorry I disappeared last week. Can I explain?"

Even though every fiber of my being wants to reach out and pull her to me, to feel her in my arms and let that be enough, I resist.

"Explain what, exactly?" I regret the biting tone as soon as the words come out. But now that I've started, I can't seem to stop. "The fact that you tore out of here because of an emergency? Yeah, I get that. Makes sense. Or maybe you want to explain why you ignored almost all of my messages for a week? Oh no, wait." I unfold my arms and stand up straight. My pain and anger are taking over. "Maybe you want to explain why you didn't want me to come to the mainland and help. Could it, I dunno, have something to do with the guy you were hugging at lunch yesterday?" Her eyes widen. I should stop talking and let her explain. I know I should. But I don't, I can't. My emotions are in control, not logic. "I saw you. See, I was on the mainland, looking for you. I realized I was a selfish fool for not being there while you cared for your dad. What kind of man does that to the woman he loves?" A harsh laugh escapes me as the words I just used sink in for both of us. "Yeah. I love you, Ashley. So imagine my surprise when I see you having lunch with another guy, when you're supposedly caring for your sick father. Now imagine that surprise cranking up a million notches when I see you hug him. What happened to *I don't like to hug people unless I'm really close to them.* Or wait, maybe you *are* really close to that guy. Maybe he's —"

"Stop! Just stop!" she yells at me, flinging her hands up. Tears are welling in her eyes.

Good. Let her suffer like I am. She's ruined me.

Chapter Twenty-Eight

Ashley

I can't believe this is happening.

Never in a million years could I have predicted something like this. Finn is so angry over something that isn't even real.

"You have to listen to me, and stop jumping to horrible conclusions," I say, swiping angrily at the tears on my cheeks. "What you saw was me having lunch with a college friend. A very happily married *to another man* college friend. He offered me a job, a partnership, here on Vancouver Island. In Westport, actually."

My chest is heaving with the emotional weight of all this. It's too much. I need to get away. But I need to tell him everything first. "I took a job here. I wanted to move here. And I was coming back to tell you I love you." My voice breaks on a sob. "How could you possibly think I would ever do anything like that? How could you question my loyalty after everything you know I've been through?"

I turn around and start to walk to my car.

"Ashley, wait." His voice sounds broken, but I ignore him and walk faster. "Ashley! Please stop!"

"Finn. No. Let her go." Pierre's voice comes out of nowhere, and I peek over my shoulder to see him holding Finn back with a hand on his shoulder. He looks at me and nods, and I quicken my steps until I reach my car. I have to wipe my tears on my sleeve again when I glance up through the windshield to see Finn gesturing toward me and Pierre shaking his head. Gunning it, I drive away from the winery. Away from the pain.

But that's the thing about pain, I guess. You can never really get away from it.

Eventually, I find myself on Main Street, parked just down from The Nutty Muffin. Mila knows I'm back in town, she told me where to find Finn. But do I want to face her now? After things went so spectacularly wrong? A knock on my window has my eyes flying open.

"Ashley?" Mila sounds worried. Slowly, I open my door, and she pulls me straight in for a hug, and for once, I let her.

"I know you don't hug, but too damn bad, I'm hugging you," she says into my shoulder, and I just nod and let my tears fall.

She pulls back after just a brief moment, and tugs me around the side of the building to a separate door. "This leads to the apartment upstairs. Go on up, I'll grab some food and come upstairs."

Numbly, I just nod and do what she says. It's obvious she knows something's up. She's the one who sent me to the winery to find Finn, so it's not a stretch for her to assume it went badly since I'm back so soon.

Oh, and my face is blotchy and swollen from crying. Can't forget that part. I make my way up the stairs and find the door unlocked. When I walk in, I find a cute studio apartment. It's furnished, and there are some fun touches that make it clear Mila's done some decorating. The sign in the kitchen says, "Pies Before Guys," and the throw pillow on the couch has a cartoon donut on it.

I sink down on the couch and pull the donut into my chest and let out a loud sigh. I'm exhausted. Not just from what happened with Finn today, but from the entire week. Hell, the entire month. The stress of making sure the tasting room was exactly as I envisioned. The tumultuous beginning to whatever you want to call my relationship with Finn. The extreme highs and lows of being with him. My dad getting sick. And today. What I thought was going to be a great day, the start of a new beginning, going down spectacularly in flames.

The door flies open and Mila comes into the apartment carrying my bags. "You're staying here, I assume, so I grabbed your stuff and locked your car." She dumps it all on the floor, then heads back outside while I'm still sitting bewildered on the couch. Moments later she's back, this time with a container that I can only hope is filled with baked goods. She takes that and places it on the counter.

"The others are on their way."

"Others?" I manage to rasp out, my voice hoarse from crying. Mila walks over to sit beside me.

"Of course. We're not letting you go through this alone."

Well, damn, that just makes me start crying again.

Pretty soon the small apartment door is opening again. Serena walks in holding a bag and a bottle of tequila. *Uh oh*. Summer follows her in with a giant bag of popcorn. Paige and Abby are also here, each carrying takeout containers.

As they come in, I give everyone a watery smile from the couch, still clutching the darn donut cushion to my chest. Mila directs them on what to do, and I just watch, feeling a little detached.

"Okay. We'll get to the main event, aka food and drink, in a minute. First of all, Ashley, we need to know what happened," Mila says gently.

"Yeah, Mila just said heartbreak red alert and that we needed to get over here fast. What's going on?" Summer adds, coming to sit beside me on the couch.

"Wait. Hold on, we need a little fortification." Mila jumps up and runs to the kitchen before coming back with the container she brought in. When she opens it, I see it's filled to the brim with brownies, cookies, and other pastries I can't identify, but it makes me realize how hollow my stomach is, regardless. She passes it around, and once everyone has something in hand, she finally turns to me. "Now. Tell us everything."

I take a deep breath, and do just that. Everything from the past week comes tumbling out, including my confusion about what Finn and I are doing, my very real fear about moving away from my dad, and then the decision to move to Dogwood Cove and be with Finn. But when I get to what happened at the winery, I lose it.

"After what my ex did to me, for Finn to even imply, just slightly, that I could lie to him or cheat on him, or whatever he thinks happened, it broke me. All the pieces I had put back together these last few months, all the hope and excitement I had over a future here with Finn, was destroyed. And I...I just...I don't know what to do now." I break down in giant, wracking sobs. The dam that held back my pain and grief has been broken, and if I thought I'd released my emotions earlier, I was wrong. This is a tidal wave, born of months of worry, heartache, and uncertainty. Most of all, it's fueled by a deep fear that what could have been the love of my life was not what it seemed.

"I'm so sorry, guys." I sniff when I eventually manage to contain myself. Taking the tissue Summer hands me, I wipe my eyes and my nose and I sigh deeply. "I want to say I could see myself staying here regardless of being with Finn or not, but now I'm not so sure."

"First of all, what the heck are you sorry for? It sounds like Finn's the one who's been a total moron here, not you," Mila replies indignantly. "And second of all, you *can* and you *will* stay here because you belong here."

Serena walks over and pushes a frothy margarita into my hands. "Agreed. We're your friends. You're one of us. Besides, this isn't the first time we've seen each other through heartbreak. And when it happened, everyone needed something different. Summer needed some space, so we got her out of town. Mila needed a girls night at the resort and Abby needed…well, truthfully, Abby was easy. She just had to realize none of us cared if she was dating her daughter's principal."

"Exactly," Mila chimes in. "What you need is to know that you're one of us now, and we've got your back. And since I'm in charge this time, you get what worked for me. Which means drunken slumber party."

"Crude as it is, Mila's catchphrase comes to mind. Chicks before dicks," Paige chimes in and I giggle in spite of my raging emotions.

"Exactly. So, the plan is, we get drunk and talk about what an idiot he is, and then tomorrow, over hangover mimosas, we'll figure out what to do to make it all better."

I want so badly to believe her, that it's as simple as a group of women — friends — figuring out a way to repair the damage done. But I'm not so sure it'll be that easy. But then, Summer does the impossible, and with one question, brings a sense of clarity and simplicity to my mind.

"Do you still love him, even after what he said and did?" Summer asks, and a hush falls over the group.

My lip trembles. "Yes. I do." I pause and think about it, letting that truth sink into me. "I do love him. Even though it kills me to think he could ever believe I would be unfaithful in any way. Especially after what my ex did to me last year. And I can sort of see how it might appear from the outside. Finn and I have both been so stupid about communication. This wasn't entirely his fault."

"Sounds like, not only do you love him, but you might be able to forgive him, too," Summer states, and I nod in agreement.

"I think I already have. He's not the only one to blame for this mess."

The silence that follows only lasts a second before Mila claps her hands together and all eyes go to her. "Okay. Here's the plan. When Finn gets his head out of his ass and comes back to grovel, which he will because he's a good guy, we'll give him hell, but forgive him. Because we're not going to let a little miscommunication get in the way of love. Right?"

I crack a smile at how she keeps saying we. And in a wobbly voice, I say, "Right."

"Excellent. Now, who wants tacos?"

CHAPTER TWENTY-NINE

Finn

I have to fix this.

Pierre had to hold me back from running after Ashley's car once the weight of my fuck up sank in. She's right. Everything she said is right. I didn't trust her; I didn't trust us. I jumped to the worst possible conclusion, and let all of my insecurities, including some I didn't even know I had, make me blind.

I know about Ashley's past. I know what her asshole ex did to her. And most importantly, I know her heart.

Pierre only let me leave after I promised him I would not go straight to Ashley. It's a hard promise to make, but I know he means well. And I know she deserves some space. Which is why I drove straight to my house, and called the one person who I know can help me fix this.

"Mom, I screwed up."

To her credit, my incredible mother doesn't say much as I tell her how spectacularly I fucked it all up. Instead, she helps me come up with a plan that I can only hope will convince Ashley not only how sorry I am, but also how much I love her.

The next morning I start to put the plan into action. Ethan texted me to ask why all of the women were at the apartment over the bakery with Ashley overnight, and I had to confess to him how wrong I had been. After he finished telling me what an asshole of an idiot I was, he agreed to help me with my plan. It took several phone calls and a couple of favours, but I think it'll work. Even if I did have to swear to Mila that I would never hurt Ashley again or I'd risk losing access to the bakery for life.

It's early enough in the year that by the time I'm ready, the sun is starting to set. After I shower and get dressed, I run around my house tidying everything. If all goes well, the best-case scenario ends with us here, together.

My brain is on autopilot as I drive to the winery. All I have left to do now is hope that she comes and that she's willing to listen to me and forgive me.

Inside the tasting room, I survey everything with satisfaction. Ashley turned this blank space into something worthy of an award-winning winery. Everything she envisioned is perfect. It's warm and inviting, with a subtle luxuriousness that says this is the place to be, without being pretentious. It's everything I want La Lune Rouge to be.

I add my finishing touches: a bottle of sparkling wine on ice and a key to my house. It might be presumptuous of me to want her to move in, but it seems the best way to show her how serious I am about the two of us moving forward. I miss waking up with her every morning and falling asleep with her every night. I want to recreate the closeness we had at the Airbnb in our real lives, not just the forced proximity we had there.

The sound of car tires on the gravel outside makes my heart start to race.

She's here.

I wait inside, putting my hands in my pockets so I don't fidget with them nervously. Everything rides on this moment. Could I be okay without Ashley in my life? Yeah, but I wouldn't be happy. I know that now.

The door opens and she steps in. Instantly a weight lifts from my heart. The first hard part is done, she came.

"Hi," she says softly, her gaze traveling around the room. I see her take in the added touches, the candles and flowers I set up.

I walk over to her slowly and help her out of her coat, draping it over the back of a chair. Taking her hand, I lead her to one of the curved, two-seater sofas she set up for a conversation area in one part of the room. It's killing me to not immediately voice my apology, but I know I need to do this right. Once she's sitting down, I take a seat beside her, still holding on to her hand. My fingers brush over her wrist, and I can feel her pulse fluttering wildly.

"Finn —"

"No, Ashley, please let me say something," I interrupt her with a gentle squeeze of my hand. She nibbles on her lip, but nods in agreement.

Taking a deep breath, I try to remember everything I wanted to say to her. "This room is what brought you into my life, so it seemed fitting this be the place where I ask you to give me another chance to have you in my life," I begin, and I see some of the tension in her shoulders soften slightly. Good. "I'm so sorry I ever doubted you. No, wait, I need to go back further. I'm so sorry I never told you how I felt, never asked you to stay, never told you I *wanted* you to stay. I was an idiot, a scared fool, and I let that stop me from telling you how important you are to me. Our relationship didn't exactly start in the traditional way, and I wouldn't change that for anything in the world. But the one thing I would take back if I could is all the times I held back from just talking to you about us and about our future. Because that hesitation, that uncertainty, that's why I fucked up and doubted you. I let my own insecurities and my own confusion break us. And now I'm just desperately hoping you'll forgive me for being so stupid and give me a chance to fix this."

When I finish, my eyes are burning. I don't remember the last time I cried, but pouring my heart out to the love of my life seems to be what triggers it. As her hand comes up to cup my cheek, I let my eyelids fall shut and let out a shuddering sigh of relief at her touch.

"Finn. There's nothing broken about us. I was scared, too, and I didn't tell you how I feel. You're not the only one to blame for all of this." She pauses and when she tugs her lower lip between her teeth, my thumb comes up to pull it free. "You hurt me, Finn, by doubting me, by not coming to me and *asking* me about what you saw. You hurt me. But Summer helped me realize that my love for you was stronger than the hurt I was feeling."

My eyes fly open to make sure I understand what she's saying, and the love I see shining from her has me hauling Ashley into my lap and crushing her to me.

"I love you, sweet girl. I love you so damn much."

"I love you, too," she murmurs against my neck. And then she's kissing me and the crack that formed in my heart watching her drive away from here yesterday is healed. Her hands go to the buttons on my shirt, and she starts to undo them. My hands find her ass and grip tightly as she starts to grind against me. When she's peeled off my shirt, Ashley's nails scrape lightly down my chest. My nipples pebble underneath her touch and my control starts to slip.

"Babe, if you don't slow down, this will be over before it starts."

She stops moving. And starts laughing.

"Was that funny?" I mock growl, making quick work of ripping her sweater off over her head.

"No," she giggles, shaking her head back and forth. "I'm sorry. It's not funny. It's just that I'm so relieved to know I'm not the only one half insane with needing to fuck right now."

"Oh goddamn, woman," I groan, "You talking dirty like that isn't helping." I stand up with her in my arms and pivot around before setting her down on the couch. The rest of my clothes end up in a pile somewhere as quickly as I can get them off, and then I'm on my knees in front of her. Slowly, reverently, I peel her pants down and off her legs until all that's left is a scrap of lace covering her.

I can smell her desire. And it ramps up my own even higher. Bending forward, I press a kiss to her lace-covered sex, feeling the rasp of the fabric against my lips. She moans, and her fingers tunnel in my hair, holding me in place. As if I would move.

"Are you attached to these?" I ask in a gravelly voice, and the adorably confused expression on her face is enough of an answer for me. I tear her panties off and while she's still gasping in surprise, I'm licking her slit from end to end, turning that gasp into a shriek.

"Ohmygod. Yes."

I let my scruff rasp along her inner thigh as I nuzzle her, breathing in the perfume of Ashley and sex. It's my favourite scent in the entire world. But what's even better is her taste. Sweeter than any wine. I spread her legs even wider, stretch one hand up to cup her breast, and I feast. Slow, fast, flicks and sucks, I know the combination of everything drives her crazy. My thumb comes to her clit, circling it with light pressure as I tunnel my tongue and use it to thrust into her.

My own arousal is sending white-hot bursts of pleasure through me, as if I'm coming close to an orgasm simply from pleasuring Ashley. It wouldn't surprise me if I did; I'm addicted to making her come.

"I'm close. I'm so close," she pants, and I double down on my efforts.

"Finn. I need you to touch me."

I growl at the sound of her demanding what she needs from me. There's nothing hotter than Ashley taking control. Rising up on my knees I lift two fingers to her mouth.

"Suck."

She pulls my fingers into her mouth and swirls her tongue around them with a moan.

"Fuck," I ground out, dropping my head to take her breast in my mouth. I bite at her nipple and tug it gently before releasing it with a pop and moving to the other side. Her hands find my shoulders and she pushes me down, and I go, chuckling at her.

"I've got you, sweet girl."

Keeping my eyes trained on her, I slide my fingers in and out of her heat. Her hips lift to meet me and I settle back down and take her clit into my mouth. Sucking on it, letting the flat of my tongue apply just the right amount of pressure, I curl my fingers up and find the magical spot that sends her flying.

When she stops crying out my name, I reach over to grab the condom I stashed in my back pocket. Rising to stand, I roll it on then hold my hand out to Ashley. We switch positions so that I'm sitting on the couch and she's straddling me again and she wastes no time in sinking down on my cock.

"Oh Lord, that feels good," she says on a sigh as I fill her up. She leans down to kiss me and her hair tickles my chest. Neither one of us is moving our hips yet, and that's okay. Just being in her like this, connected in the deepest possible way, it's enough for now.

But not for long.

Her hips start to rock against mine. My hands find her ass and I hold on, helping her lift up and down along my cock. Her hands find their way to my shoulders and she braces herself on me as her head falls back. Damn, the sight of her breasts bouncing to the rhythm of her hips is perfection.

"I'm close," she moans, dropping forward so that her hair hangs around us in a curtain.

"Good," I growl. Pistoning my hips up and down, I grip her hips tightly. Her arms wrap around my neck, pressing us together, and when I feel her clench around my cock, I come with a roar. I hear her cry out my name as her own release overtakes her seconds behind me.

Eventually, we disentangle ourselves and I go quickly to the bathroom to clean up. When I walk back into the room, Ashley is curled up on her side, squished into the small couch. "Whose idea was it to get such small furniture?" I ask sarcastically as I attempt to fit beside her. She manages to nuzzle into me some-how.

"Mine. And it was a great idea. Because these couches were not bought with sex in mind."

"Babe, always buy stuff with sex in mind." I kiss the tip of her nose, just as a loud noise erupts from Ashley's stomach and we both start to laugh. "Hungry?" I tease.

"Hey, I was too nervous about coming here, so I didn't eat lunch."

I shift so that we're on our sides, still curled up tightly on the small couch. "Then let's go home so I can feed you."

"Home?" she asks softly, and I reach my hand over to the table next to us and pick up the house key I put there.

"Yeah. Home. You already know I make a decent roommate," I say nervously, holding it in front of her.

She takes it and gives me a tremulous smile. "Are you asking me to move in with you?"

"If it means you'll stay here, with me, then yes." My voice cracks with emotion.

Ashley stands up, wearing nothing but my shirt, and moves around the room, picking up our clothes.

"Ash?" I ask hoarsely, still waiting for her to reply.

When she faces me, there's the most brilliant smile on her face. "Come on, boyfriend, you promised me dinner."

I stand up and walk over to her, cup her face, and kiss her lips.

"Say it again."

"Say what?" she asks, her eyes dancing.

"You know what."

"Boyfriend?"

"Yeah," I kiss her again. "I like that."

Epilogue

Ashley

Dating a sexy winemaker comes with a few perks. Watching him check on his grapes, backwards ball cap that never fails to make my panties wet? Just one of them.

I walk up to the man of my dreams and wrap my arms around his waist from behind.

"Hi, boyfriend," I mumble into his shirt. I feel the rumble of his chuckle and he turns around so he can hug me back. For a girl who doesn't like to hug people, I'm pretty damn sure I'm addicted to hugging him. Heck, I'm addicted to everything about him.

"Hi, girlfriend." He kisses my head and I lift my chin to face him, and he kisses my lips.

"Everyone will be here soon, I figured I should give you a bit of time to finish sweet-talking your grapes."

"You tease, but science has shown that giving plants positive attention and talking kindly to them really does help promote healthy growth."

"Uh huh, and it doesn't make you look like a crazy plant dad at all." I shake my head teasingly.

Finn drapes his arm over my shoulder as we slowly make our way to the main building of the winery. The tasting room was finished six months ago in early February. The winery opened and was an instant success. Now it's late August, and today we're hosting all of our friends for a tasting because Finn and Pierre are unveiling two of their estate wines. He's been very secretive about this, not letting me see or taste anything. I don't know if he's nervous for some reason, but he shouldn't be. I'm so proud of him. La Lune Rouge is already making a name for itself on the BC wine scene and the tasting room is booked solid every day.

An hour later, Finn has changed out of his work clothes and ditched the hat, much to my dismay. Still, the whole dressed up sommelier look is equally hot, I must admit.

The tasting room is full of conversation and laughter. Our friends are all here, Pierre's wife, my father, and even Finn's parents. It's the best kind of party, relaxed and fun. Mila has some of her staff from Camille's here to serve finger foods, and Pierre and Finn hired some people to pour wine.

I make my way over to one corner where the girls are all laughing about something. I join them just in time to hear Serena speak.

"All I'm saying is, I don't understand why it's frowned upon for women to have casual sex when it isn't for men. I need an orgasm on the regular or I get cranky."

"In my experience, an orgasm was nothing more than a light flush of heat. I suppose the process was enjoyable, but I quite frankly do not see how that could affect your mood so strongly." Paige nudges her glasses up her nose and takes a sip of her wine, oblivious to the incredulous expressions on our faces.

"That doesn't sound like much of an orgasm, Paige," Summer says. "Has it always been like that?"

"Each of the three times my partner and I came together, yes. I found the experience rather anticlimactic." Paige lifts her shoulders in a dismissive way. No one seems surprised by her lack of experience, so I say nothing. Out of everyone, Paige is still the woman I know the least.

"Oh Paige." Serena rubs her arm. "Just wait, one day some guy is gonna come and show you what it's all about. And when he does, we'll be here waiting to say I told you so."

Paige opens her mouth to respond, but we're interrupted by the clink of a glass.

"Okay, okay, can I have everyone's attention, please?" Finn's warm voice carries over the room and we turn to face him. He finds me quickly and gives me the special smile that is mine alone. "Babe, can you come up here, please?" I make my way to the bar and stand beside him. He's holding a bottle with the label facing his chest. "We invited you all here to share our first batch of estate wine. This is wine that is truly from this winery. We grew these grapes, harvested them, and turned them into something special." Finn takes a deep breath. I'm filled with so much happiness and pride for him. "What makes it even better is that one of the components used in this blend is grape juice imported from my grandfather's winery in France. We're growing those grapes right here on this land, and by this time next year we should be harvesting them ourselves. But for now, this is a damn good compromise. I promised him that someday I would bring his wine to Canada, and now I have."

The room erupts into cheers, and I see tears in the eyes of Finn's mother. But he holds up his hand to silence everyone. "There's more. This first ever batch has a special label for its debut." Finn shifts slightly to face me. "Ashley, my love, will you do the honours?"

Confused, I take the bottle. My eyes glance down to see what's different on this label compared to the mock-up he showed me last week, and a gasp of surprise escapes me. Where the logo for the winery should be are two words —

Marry Me?

"Ashley Elliott, my sweet girl. You came into my life to design this tasting room and in the end, you redesigned my future. I tried to resist you at first, for all the wrong reasons, but you were irresistible. Because you, with your throw pillows and wall sconces, are everything I need in life. I promise I will always love you, always trust you, and always tell you how much you mean to me. Most of all, I promise to always have hot sauce in the house as long as you promise to never ask me to watch a horror movie with you. Will you do me the ultimate honour of marrying me and being with me always?"

Tears are blurring my vision, making it hard to see, and I swipe them away in a hurry. Finn is on his knee in front of me, smiling hopefully, and holding the most beautiful ring I've ever seen. Trembling, I put my hand out, and he takes it, kisses the back of it, then slides the ring on. I think everyone is cheering, but I can't hear them. All of my senses are zeroed in on the man rising to his feet in front of me.

His large hands cup my face and pull me in close. I love that his eyes are shining with tears as well.

"Is that a yes?" he whispers, and I nod.

"Yes." I laugh and fling my arms around his neck. "I want to be this happy forever."

"Good. Because forever is what I had in mind."

Desperate for more Finn and Ashley? Read a spicy scene from their honeymoon by visiting https://bit.ly/JuliaJarrett_WP_bonus

ACKNOWLEDGMENTS

Every now and then, a story comes along that challenges you far more than any other. This was that book. I loved Finn the first time I met him in my head, while writing Always and Forever. I knew he had to have the sexiest story I could possibly give him. So special thanks has to go to my girl Mae Harden for sprinkling her "smut dust" and making those scenes all the better.

Like I do with every book, my undying gratitude must go to my team. Without my beta readers, Erin and Erica, my assistant Carolina, and my editor Chris, I would be nowhere, and this book would be a pile of torn up digital paper in a garbage can somewhere. Thank you thank you thank you.

To my sisters in crime, Chelle, Mae, Georgia and Claire, thank you for keeping me sane, talking me off a ledge more than once, and pushing me to be the best I can be. I love you all.

Of course I would not be here, writing these stories, without the love and support of my family. My husband, my kids, and everyone who supports me along the way. Thank you.

Also By Julia Jarrett

<u>Dogwood Cove</u>

Always and Forever

Rumours and Romance

Work and Play

Truth and Temptation

Then and Now

Passion and Promises: A Dogwood Cove Novella Collection

<u>The Donnellys of Dogwood Cove</u>

Dare To Kiss you

Hate To Want You

Pretend To Love You

Promise To Marry You

Dare To Marry You: A Donnellys of Dogwood Cove Holiday
Novella

One Night To Win You

<u>Standalone</u>

Seductive Swimmer - A standalone novel set in the Cocky Hero World, inspired by Vi Keeland and Penelope Ward's Cocky Bastard series

About Julia Jarrett

Julia Jarrett is a busy mother of two boys, a happy wife to her real-life book boyfriend and the owner of two rescue dogs, one from Guatemala and another one from Taiwan. She lives on the West Coast of Canada and when she isn't writing contemporary romance novels full of relatable heroines and swoon-worthy heroes, she's probably drinking tea (or wine) and reading.

For a complete listing of Julia Jarrett books please visit www.authorjuliajarrett.com/books

<u>Follow Julia:</u>

Instagram @juliajarrettauthor

Facebook Reader Group: Julia Jarrett's Nutty Muffins

TikTok @julia.jarrett.author